Murderer's Blade

ALLISON MOORES

MURDERER'S BLADE

A NOVEL

NEW YORK

LONDON • NASHVILLE • MELBOURNE • VANCOUVER

Murderer's Blade

A Novel

Published in New York, New York, by Morgan James Publishing. Morgan James is a trademark of Morgan James, LLC. www.MorganJamesPublishing.com

Proudly distributed by Ingram Publisher Services.

Morgan James BOGO™

A **FREE** ebook edition is available for you or a friend with the purchase of this print book.

CLEARLY SIGN YOUR NAME ABOVE

Instructions to claim your free ebook edition:
1. Visit MorganJamesBOGO.com
2. Sign your name CLEARLY in the space above
3. Complete the form and submit a photo of this entire page
4. You or your friend can download the ebook to your preferred device

ISBN 9781631957505 paperback
ISBN 9781631957512 ebook
Library of Congress Control Number:
2021945573

Cover Design by:
Karen Dimmick

Interior Design by:
Christopher Kirk
www.GFSstudio.com

Morgan James is a proud partner of Habitat for Humanity Peninsula and Greater Williamsburg. Partners in building since 2006.

Get involved today! Visit MorganJamesPublishing.com/giving-back

To Alex

ACKNOWLEDGMENTS

Writing *Murderer's Blade* was an all-consuming experience for me. I was ten years old when I started writing this book and twelve when I finished, so it's no surprise that my biggest thank you goes to my parents, who believed in me enough to let me do my own thing. They never said that I couldn't do it and never tried to interject their views into my story, although I am confident they were at times horrified by the gory scenes and the tough choices my characters often experienced. They brought me food while I was agonizing over my chapters and cleaned my hamster's cage even though I promised it would be my job. They allowed me to skip social events at my school and sometimes miss my homework assignments. Without their support, this book would not have happened.

My editor, Hannah VanVels, deserves an award for being my mentor, writing coach, and an absolute inspiration. She tirelessly and patiently held my hand and helped me to chisel and refine my story, always caring about the *Murderer's Blade* characters as much as I did. I will forever be a better writer because of Hannah.

A separate and huge thank you goes to Cortney Donelson, the associate publisher of Fiction from Morgan James Publishing, for giving me a chance and believing in me when the publishing world seemed like an impossible puzzle to navigate. The whole team at Morgan James Publishing has provided me with such incredible support. They are all masters of their trade, and I am lucky to work with each and every one of them.

CHAPTER ONE
FIRST BLOOD

SCARLET

I wait there in the dark, listening closely for the faint and familiar crack of the street camera after Kate throws her knife. When it hits the dead center of the security camera, I jump down from the roof of the apartment building. I slide down the smooth surface of the awning I have landed on. In this city, the police rest their guns unattended against the buildings, but their weapons are equipped with sensors that indiscriminately shoot anyone who walks by their aim, effectively turning entire city blocks into no-man's-lands. What the police do not know, however, is that I have been spying on them. Watching. And waiting.

I land on the ground directly in the path of the guns, and bullets begin flying through the air, most heading right toward me. I swiftly dodge and jump away before turning back to face them. I don't have a choice. This is the only way to get into the city square. And a girl's gotta do what a girl's gotta do.

But I have gotten ahead of myself. Let me tell you the full story . . .

My name is Scarlet Camper. When I was just a few months old, I was dropped off at a youth rehabilitation center, or YRC for short. There are many YRCs spread all over the country—ever since the war—and some are better than others. Most of them train abandoned kids to serve as military guards or mechanics, and this was my home until I was twelve. I can't say it was the best of childhoods, but at least I had a roof over my head. When my YRC lost its funding, I no longer had that luxury.

I was known as a rebel, and most of my teachers only tolerated my insubordination because, with all of my tardiness and bad attitude, I was the only kid who got a perfect score on every test. Ms. Fletcher was the only adult who was genuinely kind to me at the YRC. When I found myself alone in the countryside and homeless, my only hope was a referral note Ms. Fletcher wrote for me. Every time I felt like I couldn't take another step with my blistered and scabbed feet, my hand would automatically reach for the sheet of paper with the note and the map I was hurriedly able to tear out of a directory before everybody was forced to leave the building.

I remember every word Ms. Fletcher whispered to me before shoving the note in my hand. She talked about an academy in Arizona, a special, top-security program only a few people knew about. For some reason, she believed I had a shot at being accepted. A very long shot.

The address on Ms. Fletcher's note simply didn't exist. I searched every abandoned street, five blocks in every direction. Turns out there was a hidden door, which I discovered when I was seeking shelter for another sleep out in the elements. I was settling in for a cold night when I leaned against a rock. The rock tilted back as if it was going to fall over, but it stopped partway, and a door opened up to reveal a hidden room. I wasn't sure if I was hallucinating or if it was real. Maybe, I thought, it was just what my tired mind wanted to see.

When a bright glare hit my eyes, I nearly fainted. I backed away, disoriented and lightheaded.

The light was then blocked as a group of three adults, dressed in all black, emerged from inside the room. They approached me slowly, and I stood there, shocked and unmoving, still not certain if what was unfolding before my eyes was real. It was as though I was watching it play out from the perspective of an observer, like I was not an active participant in the events happening in the here and now.

I did not fight as they brought me through what seemed like endless corridors and sat me at a table. I was weak and still disoriented, so it took me a moment to register that someone was setting a plate of food before me. There was a large loaf of bread, still warm from the oven, and some fresh fruit. I quickly devoured the bread and fruit; they were delicacies to my rumbling stomach.

As strange as it sounds, having been orphaned, homeless, and alone, at that moment, I felt like I had everything in the world.

Little did I know that by stepping into that room, I was applying for school—an academy of vigilantes. An academy that only accepts the best and brightest kids, who are then trained to capture criminals that even the police are too afraid to face. Ms. Fletcher was one of their recruiters. When she selected me, the YRC was dissolved to cover any trail of my existence. I was too young to realize that so many kids lost the only home they knew just to provide another recruit for the academy.

The next few days were nothing but a blur as I was enrolled into the system of this strange school. Forty other kids, now peers, populated my classes. We met every day at an outdoor training center where we had access to a broad spectrum of weapons and training equipment: targets, punching bags, crossbows, firearms, and dueling rings. In addition to physical training and self-defense, we also learned how to negotiate with captors and hack security systems, all of which were indispensable to us as future capturers. Even though my peers had more experience in these fields than me, I easily excelled in all of our training and assignments. It was as if I was born for this. I gained weight, putting on muscle, and was nourished by a combination of eating regular meals, physical activity, the comfort of having a bed each night, and friends.

My best friend became a girl named Kate, and we started working together on our missions, which at first were just for practice. Our capture rates went up, and soon, we both qualified for the Final Four lessons. The Final Four lessons were classes in which only the top five students in the school joined. While everyone at the school undergoes basic training, the advanced lessons were specifically reserved for the most elite capturers-to-be.

Luckily, Kate and I both got in, but a boy named Justin was accepted too. Justin didn't talk much, but when he did, it was always to spout something rude, and it was always directed at me. Kate usually had my back when it came to Justin's torments, but I still avoided him whenever possible. *The piece of crap.*

During our first lesson together, we learned how to properly throw a knife through the air. Kate quickly mastered this skill because she had been studying knife-throwing since she was young. Our next class was a stealth and quick-capture class. We learned to use the infamous weapon called glare. It seemed like a lifetime ago that I had encountered the glare when I first discovered this school, or—perhaps, more appropriately—when this school first discovered me. I am a different person now. My life has been divided into a before and an after; tipping that rock was the crucial point of no return.

The next few years repeated the same grueling schedule. Early rising, late classes. Not enough sleep, absolutely no free time, and nothing for ourselves. Justin repeatedly tormented me, and Kate continued to come to my rescue, saving the day. Over and over and over again.

Until the day we finally had the opportunity to jump into action. *Until now.*

It's the day of our first real capture. I am fifteen years old now, and my life as an unruly YRC kid is long behind me. I am ready. The street camera cracks as Kate disables it with a well-placed knife throw. I jump down from the roof of the apartment building. My foot swiftly slides across the felt of the restaurant's umbrella on which I landed. Bullets whiz by me, and I'm back in the present. Welcome to my life.

We had split into teams to take on different areas of the city where hordes of criminals ran rampant. I'd partnered with Kate for this, our first capture. The person we are trying to catch is a middle-aged man who has killed many innocent people, mainly those who could not pay back the money they had borrowed to help put food on their tables for their families. Jobs are hard to come by in the present corrupt and lawless reality.

Our target always wears a beanie, and he stores a small pistol inside the rim. His whip is disguised as a belt, which he can use to choke anyone within seconds. And Kate and I are about to face him. We know he is in this neighborhood. We tracked his gun to this location, and we are close. Kate and I huddle together behind a pair of black trash bins.

"Scarlet? I don't know about this," Kate says, her knife shaking in her anxious fingers. She always wears her emotions plainly on her face when it is just the two of us, a rare vulnerability that we didn't often reveal of ourselves.

"It's just like training," I reassure her, "except we might actually die." I swallow. Maybe I'm a bit nervous myself.

"Wanna turn back?" Kate asks.

"No!" I say quickly. "Then Justin will beat us. And we need to catch this criminal, or he could kill more people!" I'm not sure I even believe myself.

"I know . . . you're right," Kate says. "It's just that—"

Suddenly, a third shadow appears before us, lurking large in the darkness.

"Oh, my gosh! Scarlet, turn around!"

I spin, pulling out my glare and flashing it. The figure stumbles back but not before one of his knives cuts Kate on the edge of her ear. She touches the blood dripping down as if she can't believe what is happening, her face stark white. I take off toward the figure, my feet pounding on the pavement after him. I pump my legs as fast as I can. Faster, faster, faster! I get close and swing at him, and he goes down hard.

"Yes!" I exalt, already feeling the success of my first capture. Until I realize it's Justin.

"What the heck?" Justin groans from the ground, his eyes still adjusting from the extreme brightness of the glare.

"Good grief, Justin! We thought you were someone else. What are you doing here?" I don't reach out a hand to help him as he struggles to get back up, clearly disoriented. Kate approaches us, blood dripping down her cheek.

"Kate!" Justin perks up. "Oh, no, Kate! Did I . . . did I get you? I—I'm so sorry," Justin stammers, and I roll my eyes.

"I will forgive you for cutting me if you forgive us for tackling you," Kate says, looking him in the eye. I'm grateful she included herself in the "us" and smile at her.

"Yes! I forgive you and . . . Scarlet," Justin says, struggling to say my name.

"Alright. Go do your own plot." Kate points to the dark alley connecting the streets. "Go! We are working here."

She and I watch Justin leave, and I feel a twinge of satisfaction as I notice his slight limp. I must have tackled him pretty hard. He had it coming.

Kate and I continue waiting, counting the seconds, minutes, hours that go by on our watches. Still no sign of our target. We're walking around the dark square, looking for any signs of our guy when a shadowy figure appears in the square we just entered. Not this again.

"Justin, stop it! We know it's you!" I shout, clenching my fists. Can't he take a hint? He already potentially messed up our plot, and if he ruins this capture for me, I will give him what he deserves.

But then this figure turns toward us and speaks in a low and muffled voice. It's then I notice the beanie with the oddly shaped bump protruding from it. And the belt that's a bit narrower on one side than the other.

"Well, hello there, *children*. What are you doing out so late? Where are your mommy and daddy?" he says, his voice harsh.

"Oh, no," Kate whispers to me frantically. "It's him."

"I know." I try to use the glare, shining the light in his eyes. He jumps out of the way, then masterfully uses a built-in shield on his sleeve to reflect the light back at Kate. She falls, shielding her eyes, immobilized for the moment. He's done this before, I figure.

I throw electric darts at the man, but he dodges every single one. How is this guy so agile? Kate hurls her knives at him, and even under stress, I'm impressed that her aim is still amazing, despite being disoriented and half-blind. Once more, though, he leaps away, unscathed, and carefully moves toward us. This is all going terribly wrong. How could we have let ourselves get so lazy? How did we not see his approach?

"Wait, Kate!" I say, an idea popping into my head. "Put your gas mask on!" She obeys, and I retrieve from my pocket a small canister of gas that precipitates a loss of consciousness when it's inhaled.

"Hey, you! Why do you keep running away?" I shout at him. He growls at me and lunges, brandishing a small gun. I spray the chemical in the direction of our attacker, and it works. He is caught off-guard and stumbles through the thick cloud of gas before he can reach us, collapsing a few feet away from where we stand, unconscious.

I approach him cautiously and take out my handcuffs. Cuffing him while he's still unconscious, I call in reinforcements. The man begins to stir and comes to his senses, but it is already too late. He has been captured. Our first.

"Yes! We've completed our first mission," I say.

Kate takes off her gas mask and is smiling ear to ear. "We did it, Scarlet! And we didn't die!"

We wait until our captive is picked up and brought back to our headquarters, which is hidden in the mountains. Then, we receive our grade from the head of the school for our assignment. We are the first and only group to have successfully completed our mission. Everyone is waiting back inside the main office. Some of our peers look a bit battered and bruised, but everyone, including Justin, congratulates us.

We had won. I smile at Kate. We are an unbeatable team. We knew we could do this.

But what we didn't know was that the murderer has accomplices.

Chapter Two
NEW RECRUIT

SCARLET

When Kate and I return to our dorm, we both fall asleep almost immediately, our adrenaline rush having been entirely depleted and replaced by deep exhaustion. Before I know it, and much too soon, my alarm is blaring at me.

BEEP! BEEP! BEEP! BEEP!

I groan into my pillows and fumble to turn it off. I know that despite last night's victory, today will not be a day for relaxing. Our trainers will go no easier on us for our successful performance last night. There will be no high fives, congratulatory slaps on the back, or celebratory words.

No, today our trainers will push us even harder. There is no exceeding expectations at this academy. There is only hard work.

Kate and I blearily walk into the training center, pale-faced and puffy-eyed. Although we are deep within a mountain hideout, I know the sun is only beginning to rise. I stifle a yawn as we approach our two instructors who are waiting for us.

"Today, we will begin private lessons," Instructor Sanchez says without any greeting or preamble. "Advanced weapons, advanced techniques, and advanced intelligence. Your success last night on your mission indicates that you are ready for this next step." She stares at us, and her stern brown eyes seem to absorb all the light in the room. I resist a nervous gulp and throw a half-glance at Kate, unsure of what to expect. "Welcome to Captures."

I blink, and before I can help myself, I blurt out, "*Captures*, Instructor?" *Crap.* I shouldn't have said anything, but to my surprise, Instructor Sanchez smiles at me.

"You are being trained to capture criminals and take them into custody. Surely, you have realized that by now?" Instructor Sanchez adds with a raised eyebrow.

"Oh" is all I say. I feel stupid for saying anything at all. I need to learn how to keep my mouth shut.

"Now, grab those javelins," Instructor Sanchez says, "and let's get started."

This becomes our routine. Kate and I attend our private classes every day, and every morning, Justin glares at us as we walk into a different training room than him and the rest of the Four. I don't bother hiding my smirk from him. He is clearly jealous and angry since he has not passed his plot yet. Green is a great color for him, and I relish every one of his envious glances. *That's right*, I want to say to him, *I'm beating you*.

I whisper quietly to Kate as he walks by, "Maybe next time he will focus on his own mission instead of ours." Kate gives a small nod, staring at Justin's back with a strange look on her face. Justin steps into his own training room instead of following us to our elite training lessons. I glance back at Kate, and my next takedown dies in my throat.

"Quit staring, Kate! We will be late for combat training," I say instead, nudging her. I glance down at the watch on my wrist and am startled to see that I'm not entirely wrong. We only have a few minutes before our training is scheduled to begin, and our room is clear across the school.

"Okay, okay, sorry! Jeez," Kate hisses back. She grabs my arm. "C'mon, let's go."

We weave through the masses of people crowding the hallways, the other students and the faculty at the school. We break through the crowd and jog down a maze of hallways leading to various classrooms and training rooms. When we arrive at our room, we are a whole minute late.

"You're late," our teacher, Instructor Huang, says coldly, glaring at us. I open my mouth to apologize, but before I can speak, she pulls out a timer and continues. "You know what that means. Pushups! I'm feeling benevolent so only one hundred this time. Well, what are you waiting for? Go! Go! Go!"

Kate and I jump and run to the mat that takes up most of the room. We drop to the ground and start our punishment. I can't help but feel irritated at Kate for her lingering look at Justin, though I know my feelings are irrational. It was probably nothing, and I'm reading too much into it. I know my best friend. My arms and shoulders burn, and my core feels too tight with every up and down of my body. Instructor Huang stands over us, counting down each movement. When we finish, Kate and I collapse on the mat, both panting. A hand reaches out to help me up, and I gratefully take it.

"Thanks, Instructor," I say instinctively. But when I look up at who I am grabbing onto, it is not Instructor Huang.

It's a boy I have never seen before standing there instead, my hand clasped in his. Even in my shock, I can't help but notice his stunning brown eyes, dark and full, with veins of amber and gold running through them. "Uhh . . . hi there, I'm Ryan. Ryan Pentaquese," he says, looking down at me. "W—what's your name?"

"Scarlet," I answer quietly.

"Scarlet," he says slowly, as if tasting, savoring the sounds of my name. "I like that name." His eyes crinkle in a kind smile, and I notice a dimple on one of his cheeks. He runs a hand through his dark curls. "It was nice to meet you, Scarlet. I'm just dropping off a note for Instructor Huang. I will be seeing you." He smiles at me again, and that dimple makes my head swirl. I realize I am blushing fiercely.

"Ooooooh! I think someone likes you!" Kate says from the floor, grinning from ear to ear.

"Well, what about you and Justin?" I snip, embarrassed and annoyed that my face is still flushed.

"We're talking about you, Scarlet," Kate protests, irritated, as she stretches on the mat. "That's beside the point. Ryan was totally flirting with you. And did you see those gorgeous eyes?"

"Uhh, Kate? I get that you missed out on your childhood dreams, but this is stupid," I say, rolling my eyes.

"Ohh, I see. You like him too!" she says smugly. "Scarlet and Ryan' has a cute ring to it, huh? I mean, he is very cute."

"Shut up!" I respond, grabbing her roughly by the shoulders, unable to keep the flush from brightening my cheeks. "Okay, okay, he's cute. Whatever."

"Boxing ring! Now!" Instructor Huang hollers at us before we can discuss my love life any further. I am grateful for her timing.

As Kate and I wrap our hands up and practice our punches and footing, I can't keep Ryan's face from creeping into my mind. Those amazing eyes and that dimple. And the firm, warm grip of his hand in mine. I am head over heels for this pair of big, brown eyes that I've just met. I'm not sure how I feel about it. I never thought much about the concept of love at first sight, but maybe that's what this is. Honestly, I never thought much about love in any way, whether at first sight or not. My life has always been just me since living at the

YRC and for as long as I can remember. I've never considered what it might be like to have a boyfriend. I suppose dating is a normal part of being fifteen, but what part of my life has ever been normal?

Kate aims a punch at my face, and I duck out of the way. A whistle sounds, and Instructor Huang steps in to correct Kate's posture. I lower my arms.

Maybe it wouldn't be so bad to embrace this normal part of being a teenager. Maybe it wouldn't be so bad to talk to Ryan again and see where things go. And if Kate is wrong about Ryan being interested in me . . . well, I've been alone most of my life. I will be fine.

At the end of our combat lesson, Kate and I leave together, sweaty and aching from a grueling workout.

"Remind me to set my watch five minutes ahead. I cannot take another round of pushups before boxing," Kate says to me as we make our way into the crowded hallway toward the academy's cafeteria. "I think my arms might fall off."

Just then, I spot those familiar dark curls that have been occupying my thoughts for the past two hours. "I will catch up to you, Kate," I say distractedly. I push past a few people and catch up to Ryan, who is walking to his classroom with two other members of the Final Four.

"Ryan!" I call, and he turns. "Um, hi. We meet again so soon," I say awkwardly. My insides feel as though they are withering. Dang it, I should have thought of something cool to say.

"Scarlet," Ryan replies with a gentle smile. Under the fluorescent lights of the hall, his eyes look nearly black, as if they attract and absorb all the light that touches him. I am a moth attracted to them, being pulled in by his dark gaze.

"I like your smile," I blurt out. *What the heck?*

Ryan awkwardly runs his hands through his curls and looks down at his feet. "Really? No one's ever told me that before," he tells me, as though what I had just said was somehow a completely normal thing to say to a guy you've just met.

At this point, I am blushing furiously. I'm so glad Kate isn't here to witness this. *Get yourself together, Scarlet,* I chide myself.

"So . . . when did you join our class?" I ask wildly, desperate for a change of topic.

"My brother goes here. His name is Jack," Ryan says. "It seems we have a long line of relatives who went here as well."

"Did you just join the Final Four today?" I ask curiously.

"Yeah, I just joined the academy today actually. I don't think I would have minded being in regular classes to start, though, because now Jack is really jealous that I got to skip basic training altogether. The only upside is I guess I get to see you every day, huh? Sorry, am I rambling?" He is definitely rambling.

"Just a little bit," I say with a smile, trying to be polite, mostly because I like him but also partly because he keeps covering up my own socially awkward blunders.

Without thinking, I reach out to grab his hand before I realize what I am doing. I quickly drop my hand and hide it behind my back. Ryan is kind enough to pretend not to have noticed my sudden movement, or at least, he has resolved not to mention it. We awkwardly stand in silence for a few moments before Ryan finally blurts out, "You're really nice, Scarlet." His deep brown gaze meets my own, and my heart hammers in my chest. My limbs tingle and my stomach twists itself into knots as I drink in the intoxicating swirls of the colors in his eyes.

His watch beeps, and the spell is broken. Ryan gives me a final look and heads into his classroom without another word. I stand there for a moment, piecing together what just happened. "Bye, Ryan!" I call back to him, slightly breathless. He turns toward the door, toward me, and grins, his dimple making me melt inside, and waves at me.

I slowly walk backward from his classroom door, oblivious to the curious stares of his classmates and the other students around me. I turn back only when he cannot see me and practically skip to my room, a squeal bursting to leave my chest. I have never felt so alive. I cannot contain the giant smile on my face. It stretches so far that my cheeks hurt.

Kate is waiting for me once I get back to the room, having skipped lunch, and immediately starts interrogating me, demanding answers. "Told you so, didn't I?" she teases me when I stubbornly refuse to tell her anything.

I fall back on my bed and pull my pillow over my face when suddenly, a soft object hits me in the stomach. I move my pillow aside, and Kate is standing over me, holding her own pillow in her hands, a mischievous look on her face. "I need some details, Scarlet!" she says, holding her pillow up threateningly.

I sigh in exasperation, but I can't help the smile still plastered over my face. "Okay, okay," I relent. Kate squeals and plops down on the bed next to me.

"Tell me everything!" she says, leaning forward and giving me her full and undivided attention. "Start at the beginning."

And despite my initial stubbornness, I begin to dish, even telling her about my awkward attempts at small talk because, after all, Kate is my best friend. Her face mirrors the excited grin on my own as I finish recounting my conversation with Ryan.

"So, did you make plans to see him again?" Kate asks me.

"I . . . I don't know. It didn't come up," I answer. And then my heart sinks a little and a balloon deflates inside my stomach. "We didn't make any plans," I tell her.

Kate takes my hand in hers, her eyes still bright. "Well, that's okay. You said he was in the Final Four now, so we will see him around. You can make plans to meet up when you run into each other again," she says.

But now, I'm beginning to have second thoughts. Maybe I've read too much into the situation with Ryan. Maybe I've overanalyzed what transpired between us and imagined any sparks. After all, as students of Capture, we're literally trained to analyze everything. What if I was seeing things that weren't there? What if the chemistry between us, which I felt so strongly and that practically sizzled through my body, was all in my head? Because surely, we would have made plans to hang out at least. And he said I was nice. I mean, puppies are nice too, and you wouldn't want to date a puppy. I'm being stupid and silly to jump headfirst into this new space of dating, especially with a guy I just met this morning! Even if he did have what looked to be the softest curls and the dreamiest eyes and, goodness, that dimple.

I moan and sink back into my bed, covering my face with my pillow again. "Oh, man, did I mess things up before they've even begun, Kate?" I groan through my pillow. She squeezes my knee comfortingly.

Just then, a knock sounds on the door to our dorm room. I feel Kate rise to answer it, but before she gets to the door, a voice on the other side sounds. "Scarlet? Are you in there?"

It's Ryan.

I jolt up, and my pillow goes flying across the room. Kate freezes halfway to the door and turns to me, startled.

"Uh, come in," I call loudly. I turn to Kate and hiss, "Get out!"

Kate dives into the bathroom just as Ryan enters our dorm room.

"Hey," he says as he walks in. "I hope you don't mind me stopping by. I just got out of class."

"Um. No problem," I say, fidgeting with my blankets and noticing the pillow I had flung across the room with a twinge of embarrassment. "Um. Have a good class?"

"Thank you for making my day just a little bit better," he tells me, ignoring my feeble attempt at small talk.

My mouth is dry, and I don't know what to say. I stand up to fetch the pillow on the floor. "Oh, um. Sure. Sorry for earlier." *Scarlet, why are you apologizing?* "For, you know, being so awkward. I was just afraid—"

"It's okay," Ryan interrupts, taking another step toward me. "Really, don't apologize."

"You're really nice too," I say to the pillow in my hands. I chance a look up at Ryan's face and am pleased to see him smiling. He has such a handsome smile that lights up his whole face.

Then, he reaches behind me, his arms extended, and it's as if everything is happening in slow motion. Before I know it, I'm in his arms, and I'm wrapping my arms around his muscled back and breathing him in. This feels so perfect, being enveloped by him, and his curls brush against my face. They are softer than I could have imagined, and I think I might faint.

Then I realize that he was actually just reaching for the door. Not reaching for a hug. *Oh. My. Gosh.*

"Oh. Um," he says and walks out of the room. He flashes me one final smile during this moment that feels like forever as he leaves.

I don't know how long I stare at the door, rooted to the spot where I'm standing and completely mortified. I forget about Kate hiding in the bathroom and slowly walk to the cafeteria for lunch. Thankfully, since it's now early afternoon, the cafeteria is fairly empty, and I sit at a table alone, picking at my pizza, thinking about Ryan for a long while. Maybe dating just isn't for me, I decide, as I dump my cafeteria tray off on the way to class. Maybe people like me are meant to be alone.

I trudge to my afternoon class, hardly paying attention to where I'm going, my feet carrying me there on muscle memory alone.

"Good afternoon, Ms. Camper," Instructor Aarons says to me as I enter the classroom.

"Good afternoon, sir," I mumble, avoiding any eye contact and slumping into a desk. A minute later, Kate prances in, smiling and skipping and greeting the teacher overenthusiastically. I know this happens to be her favorite class, but something strikes me different about her right now. She tosses her hair and smiles broadly at me. Kate is definitely acting overly sweet to everyone around her, especially considering I forgot about her hiding in the bathroom before lunch. I slump even lower in my chair, ashamed. Hopefully, she will forgive me for that. I make a note to talk to her about it later.

Consumed with my thoughts about Ryan and about Kate being weird, I struggle to focus on today's class. Instructor Aarons goes on and on, and I stare at my blank notebook page, not even focused enough to doodle absently. First, my mortifying experience with Ryan today, and now, Kate is acting so strangely. Is she mad at me for earlier? Heaven knows I probably deserve that, shoving her into the bathroom so I could have alone time with Ryan, despite the disaster *that* turned out to be. When class ends, Kate skips off out the door before I can check in with her, so I head to my next training session alone, my mind whirling.

When the day is finally over, I head back to my dorm room, mentally rehearsing my apology to Kate for forgetting about her. I enter our room. Kate is sitting at her desk, reading a book about nature. I stop dead in my tracks. Kate never reads books. Not unless it's for an assignment. I knew something was wrong earlier today when she was acting overly happy in class, but now, seeing this, my suspicions are confirmed. Something is *definitely* wrong with her.

"Scarlet!" Kate beams at me from her desk as she clutches her nature book. "Justin asked me out!" Kate says, with a big cheesy smile.

A dull roaring noise fills my ears. That piece of crap, Justin. How dare he come for my best friend to get to me? What kind of absolute moron uses someone as nice as Kate just to get at someone he hates? Because that's got to be why he's doing it. Right? My eye starts to twitch and a vein throbs painfully in my temple. Kate is still grinning at me, waiting for my response.

"Oh. Good for you!" I reply, forcing a happy enthusiasm into my voice. After a few hours of her rambling on about what comes next, she literally falls asleep in the middle of a sentence. *Finally*, I think, relieved, and look at the clock. Time for me to get some rest as well after an eventful day.

When we wake up the following morning, Kate continues on as if she had never stopped despite the fact that it's been several hours. The vein in my temple throbs in a now-familiar tempo.

"Kate," I interrupt her. "Let's get to class. We don't want to be late again. Pushups, remember?" I interrupt, pointing at the dresser so she will change and get ready to leave.

"Yeah, yeah," She waves me off. "Oh! Maybe the four of us can double date!" Kate says to me, an earnest smile on her face.

"The four of us?" I raise an eyebrow at her.

"You know," she says slyly. "Me and Justin, and you and Ryan!"

"You were talking about Justin for four hours last night!" I say hoarsely. "Let's go!" I wave my hands in the direction of the door. Despite my words, I'm in no hurry to get to class. This is training with the Final Four, and I know Ryan will be there. I am in no hurry to face him again after my embarrassing debacle yesterday afternoon.

"You don't have to be so grumpy," Kate grumbles as she jogs down the hall to catch up to me.

When we arrive at our training room, we immediately begin so there is no time for socializing. I jog around the track, watching Ryan from across the gym as he jumps rope. So far, he has not said a word to me or looked at me or acknowledged my presence in any way. I stare at him the entire lesson, expecting some kind of small gesture of social acknowledgment, anything that will show me he is still interested in me or at the very least, that I am not invisible. *Maybe I really did die of embarrassment yesterday, and now I'm a ghost, invisible to everyone*, I think feebly. When class comes to an end, Ryan bolts toward the door. It seems obvious now that he is avoiding me. Before I can sink further into my shame, I grit my teeth and speed after him. If he wants to be a jerk to me, fine, but I can't take this not knowing business.

"Hey!" I call to him, grabbing his shoulder. "What is your deal? You could at least say hello!" I yell at him. He turns around and looks at me. To my surprise, he looks panicked, and his eyes dart around the hallway.

"Leave me alone," he whispers. "You have to leave me alone, Scarlet." And he wriggles out of my rough grip and runs down the hall.

What is going on?

Chapter Three
THE BODY

SCARLET

Back in our bedroom, Kate is waiting for me. She looks up at me from her bed and immediately gets up and gives me a hug. I stand stiffly until she lets go.

"What's going on? Did something happen with Ryan?" she asks me.

I can't talk about it. I am too confused to even process my own feelings let alone talk about it out loud with Kate, though I know she means well. I ignore her question and fall into my own bed, burying myself in my pillow so she can't see my face. I feel stupid for even being upset. I mean, I barely even know the guy. But I can't shake the upset feelings. Did I do something? Was it something that I said? Why did he look at me that way? Tears begin to bubble out of my eyes and soak into the fabric of my pillowcase.

The bed sinks down as Kate sits next to me, and I feel her hand rubbing warm, comforting circles on my back.

"Scarlet? Are you okay?" she asks me.

My head remains resolutely in my pillow.

"You can talk to me, okay? I will be here when you're ready," she says. Kate sits on my bed next to me for a while, and I feel her support and solidarity in the comforting patterns her hand makes across my back. She is a good friend. Eventually, I begin to drift off, and I feel Kate get up off my bed. The absence of her weight and her warmth next to me brings me back to the present. I hear the door to our dorm shut quietly, and I know I am alone.

After a moment, I sit up. The room is dim now. Kate must have turned off the lights to let me sleep before she left. I catch my reflection in the mirror atop my dresser. My skin is pale and my eyes are red and puffy. It's obvious I've been crying. I wonder what went wrong with Ryan. We were getting along just fine until this morning. Maybe his brother said something to him to cause his sudden change. Maybe that's just who Ryan is and the Ryan that I thought I knew doesn't even exist. I truly don't know. Whatever it is, I am over it.

I stare at my bloodshot eyes in the dim mirror, and suddenly, I feel angrier at Ryan than sad. How dare he? Being nice to someone and then flipping a switch and being rude to them is not okay, and I will not allow him to treat me that way, I decide. I'm going to visit Ryan and demand answers.

Getting up, I walk over to our shared bathroom and head to the sink. I turn on the faucet and splash cold water onto my face, washing away the salty tear tracks that stain my cheeks. I pull my messy hair back in a ponytail and grab a hoodie on my way to the door.

Ryan's door is slightly ajar when I approach, as if he was expecting visitors or waiting for someone. Was he waiting for me? I knock softly on the door. "Ryan?"

"Go away," he mumbles from inside.

I tentatively push the door open and enter his dorm room. Ryan is sitting on his bed, staring intently at the wall.

"Ryan?" I call to him again. "It's me, Scarlet." Though he obviously already knows this, it feels like I should announce my presence since his eyes haven't left the wall. "Is . . . is something wrong?" I ask nervously. Although I came in here with rage boiling in my veins and had rehearsed how I would go about yelling at him for being such a jerk to me earlier, his slumped posture makes me second-guess myself.

"It's just . . ." Ryan begins. "Oh, never mind! You wouldn't understand."

I don't know what to say or how to respond. I open my mouth to speak but close it again, uncertain what words might get him to talk, or if I even want to hear what he has to say. I came here expecting to ream him out for being a jerk to me, but now that he's acting all vulnerable and sweet. All of the words I can think of seem inadequate. I chew on the inside of my cheek and simply stare at his profile as he continues to gaze resolutely at the blank wall.

"Meet me tomorrow in the locker room at 2:30 p.m.," he says suddenly.

"I . . . what?" I stutter, caught off-guard by his outburst, and then I reprimand myself.

"Isn't that during class?" I ask. *During class!* Golly, what a stupid thing to bring up.

"Exactly," Ryan says. "I can't let my family see me talking to you."

And then he finally turns away from the wall and looks at me, and the sleeping butterflies in my stomach wake up and flutter in a lively tempo.

I swallow. "Your family? What do they have to do with anything?"

"I will explain tomorrow," he says quickly.

My anger flares back up at this. "Tomorrow?" I protest. "Ryan, you're being really weird and kind of rude. I think you should explain now. What is your deal?" I cross my arms across my body self-consciously. "If I did something or if you're mad at me for some reason, I'm sorry. But you can't just keep running away from me or putting me off like this. I am a person with feelings, you know!" Too late I realize I'm practically shouting and anyone passing by in the hallway might hear me. *Well, he deserves it, to be quite honest.*

"Mad at you?" Ryan repeats, clearly confused, and his eyebrows disappear into his mess of curls. "Why would I be mad at you?" he says blankly.

It takes all my willpower to not scream at him. "I don't know," I say in a surprisingly even tone. "That is why I'm here. You tell me."

Ryan looks around nervously as if checking for hidden cameras in his room. "I can't. I will explain everything tomorrow, okay? It will all make sense. Will you be there? Will you meet me and just hear me out?"

I consider him for a moment, sitting there on his bed, imploring me with his large puppy-dog eyes. "Whatever," I say. Without another word, I turn and leave his room.

I hear him call my name, but I keep walking, and I don't look back.

And although I'm furious right now—so angry at him for keeping secrets and treating me like a second thought—and I cannot believe he still won't explain himself, I know I will show up tomorrow at 2:30 in the locker room. How could I not? His kindness seems so genuine, and his earlier indifference was so obviously forced. Or is that just my wishful thinking? I need answers.

When I arrive at my room, I find dresses everywhere. *What the heck?*

Then I remember: it's Kate's date tonight. I had completely forgotten. I peek into the bathroom and see Kate posing in a posh pink dress, a barrette decorated with royal blue gems fused into a silver flower is holding up a chic messy bun. Her dress is embroidered with designs of flowers and leaves, and the belt on the dress is a plain pink fabric that balances out the intricate pattern of the dress.

Kate opens a drawer and pulls out a pearl choker, which she fastens around her neck, and completes the look with a quick layer of lip gloss. She catches my reflection in the mirror and flushes.

"Oh. Hi, Scarlet!" she says brightly. I wonder if she's embarrassed that she's going out tonight despite my sour mood from earlier. "How long have you been there for? Did you hear me say anything? If you did——"

"No, I just got here. And you look amazing!"

"You really think so?" Kate smiles, opening up her arms and looking down admirably at her outfit. "I still can't believe he asked me out! I mean, of course, I knew he liked me, but I never thought he would ask me out. I can't believe it's tonight! I'm so excited, but I'm also really nervous . . ."

Uh oh. She's getting into her anxious boy zone, and if I don't cut her off quickly, she could go on about this for hours. I clear my throat loudly.

"Kate," I say firmly, "shouldn't you be leaving now?"

"Oh, yeah," Kate says. "I do need to go now; otherwise, I'll be late. I don't want to show up late and make him wait. Ugh! What if he's one of those people who considers showing up fifteen minutes early on time and anything after that late?"

"Kate," I repeat her name in an attempt to ground her and head her off. "I'm sure you'll be fine. After all, he obviously already likes you."

"I know, I know. When we had that long and interesting conversation about him the other night, though, I told you that he might not like me as much if he gets to know me. You remember?" Kate eyes me suspiciously, and I squirm a bit. Her eyes narrow, then she looks up at me with a playful smile and says, "Well, I better get going! Toodles!" She blows me a kiss as she moves toward the door of our dorm room.

"Okay, bye! Now leave! Go!" I say, quickly tapping her back so she will walk out. She waves at me from the hallway, and I shut the door behind her. I lean against the door and press my ear against it. I hear her footsteps fading and sigh in relief. I can finally relax now.

Even though tomorrow, I will clear stuff up with Ryan, I still cannot help but wonder what went wrong with him. I take off my clothes and get in the shower as if it will wash off all the day's events and let me rewind time to earlier today. I turn the faucet and close my eyes and step into the shower, hoping the icy water can numb my feelings. Before the water hits my head, I feel my feet slide out from under me, something thick and slimy coating my body when I hit the floor with a thud. *What the . . .*

As I open my eyes, I see the bottom of the shower covered in blood. I look up and see a steady drip of thick red liquid coming from the vent directly above the shower. As water droplets fall down from the showerhead, they create little individual craters in the deep red coating, until the color gets diluted more and more as the bloody water fails to drain. Dark red blood coats my skin, soaks into my hair, and drips down my body in an intricately morose pattern.

What in the world? I jump back. *Is this real blood?* It sure feels sticky and slick as I rub my fingers together. I start to freak out, but then my training kicks in. Rule number one is to recognize the situation. I have to recognize and suppress the panic that is building up and scrambling my thoughts. Only then can I use logic to decipher the level of threat. If somebody was trying to kill me, I'd already be dead. My skin didn't burn from the contact with the blood, so there is no immediate chemical threat, but it is still a biohazard.

Now there is blood everywhere. Shower water continues to hit the basin and splatters it all over, including on my shocked face. I wrinkle my nose and reach in to shut the faucet off, grateful for the brief contact with clean water, which rinses some of the blood from my head. I reach for my towel to wipe my face and catch my reflection in the mirror. There is blood in my hair staining the light strands red and clumping it together in thick, sticky bunches. I keep expecting that someone will burst through the door to announce an emergency, but nothing happens. Nobody is coming to fight me, kill me, or rescue me for that matter.

I curse and stick my whole head under our bathroom sink to try to rinse the blood out. *Whatever. This will have to be good enough.* I put my clothes back on and put a hat over my wet hair. I grab a bandana and a small flashlight and stuff them into my pocket. These will come in handy later. My temper rages. All of the sadness and confusion that I felt earlier is overwhelmed by irritation and anger as I am convinced more and more that this was a prank. My money is on that little weasel, Justin. Gosh, I hate him. *Is he using Kate to get to me? She will be devastated if he doesn't show up for their date!*

I slam open the door to my dorm room with a little more gusto than I mean to and stomp out to go check the vent pipe connected to our bathroom. When we were initiated, we were given tours of the entire school, and I'm not talking about just the classrooms, training rooms, and grounds. Nope. This tour included the less savory aspects of the school, such as the dark, moldy basement that houses the heaters connected to the school-wide vent system, which is where I'm headed now.

The basement corridors are murky and damp. I flick on my flashlight and examine the pipes with its dim light. I squint, trying to locate the one that leads to our room. I walk down a little deeper into the sewers, and there! Found it! And then I nearly faint in shock.

The vent cover is broken, and when I squeeze myself into the vent tunnel and follow it for two very tight and uncomfortable turns, I see a mangled human body, which looks to have been hastily shoved there. The pool of blood in my shower is coming from this poor guy. *Oh, my word! What in the world is going on?*

I slowly back away from the sick scene until I bump into a wall behind me. I scramble out and begin running down the corridor. I'm sure I'm past the door I used to enter the basement, but I continue running as fast as I can. I need to go to the headmasters, or someone, and tell them what I have found.

My lungs burn, and I pump my arms harder as I see light above me. I must have followed the underground basement all the way outside the school building. I skid to a stop and throw myself up the ladder and push open the manhole cover above me. I sprint back to the school and race to the administrative wing. Flinging the door to the headmasters' office open, I hurtle myself inside.

The three headmasters stare at me. If they are surprised, they do not show it. They merely consider me under their noses as I put my hands on my knees, trying to catch my breath.

"Headmasters," I gasp, practically wheezing at this point. I realize that I'm still caked with dried blood. "I . . . there's been an accident. In the sewers or something! A body!" In the back of my mind, I know I'm not doing a great job explaining myself.

"Miss Camper," Headmaster Samuelson says calmly. "Please, sit." She gestures to a couch in the office. I obediently sink into the couch. "Now, start at the beginning." Another headmaster hands me a bottle of water, and with shaky hands, I unscrew the cap and take a swig.

From the beginning. Where do I even start? Is Ryan's strange behavior worth mentioning?

"I was taking a shower," I begin, deciding to skip the Ryan parts of this story, "and there was blood dripping from the vent. Lots of it."

"Are you injured?" Headmaster Samuelson said, gazing at me over her glasses.

"No, I'm fine—"

"Was it your blood that could have been in the shower, Miss Camper? Perhaps you cut yourself?" Headmaster Samuelson suggested, still looking at me sternly.

"I wasn't injured. It wasn't my blood. That's what I'm trying to tell you. The blood was coming through the vent."

The three headmasters exchange doubtful looks between them.

"So I went to the basement to investigate, thinking maybe somebody was playing a prank or something. I'm not sure what I expected to see." I explain about the corpse and that I suspect the blood is coming from it. *It!*

"I can show you where it is. You can see it for yourselves," I add as the headmasters again look at each other, and I'm convinced they have their own nonverbal language. I'm not sure they believe me. Even to my own ears, the story sounds ludicrous.

They exchange another glance and Headmaster Samuelson says, "Lead us, Miss Camper."

We exit the office in a line, and I retrace my steps back to the basement. I lead them toward the body. I can make out the broken vent cover from thirty feet away in the dark. "It's

. . . there." I point. I make a move to lead them closer, but Headmaster Samuelson throws out her arm, blocking me.

"Headmaster Jeong," she says, not taking her eyes off the open vent tunnel ahead of us. "Will you please escort Miss Camper back to her dorm room?"

Headmaster Jeong nods wordlessly and takes me by the arm back down the corridor. "Come on, Miss Camper." I don't protest and allow myself to be steered away. At this point, I feel so drained of energy, both physically and emotionally, that all I want to do is take a real shower and wash this whole awful day away.

Headmaster Jeong and I walk in silence back to my dorm, and at my door, I turn to him and awkwardly say goodnight. He merely nods and leaves. With an exhausted sigh, I step into my room. With a jolt to my stomach, I remember I can't take a shower to clean up because my shower is where this mess started in the first place!

That's when I notice the lights are dim, and Kate and Justin are watching a movie together in her bed.

"Hi, Scarlet!" Kate calls from over Justin's shoulder. "Want to join us? We're watching—oh, my gosh, Scarlet!" Ah. She must have noticed the blood splattered all over my clothes. "What the heck happened?"

"Um . . . long story. Oh, and do not go into the bathroom," I say urgently as I trudge toward the morbid scene. Justin is just lounging there next to her, still watching the movie as if I wasn't even there. I'm convinced he's somehow behind this, but I can't read him. Does he know his crime has been uncovered? If he doesn't, what will he do when he finds out? I decide to wait him out and talk to Kate after he leaves.

Kate gives me a questioning look. "Scarlet, is everything okay? What's going on?" she asks me.

"Just one second!" I say, holding up a finger and stepping into the bathroom, shutting the door behind me.

Wow! It is a mess in here. I grab towels to wipe up the blood that's spilled onto the floor. The coppery odor of blood fills my nostrils, and I heave over the bathroom sink. *Yech!*

For the second time that day, I splash cold water on my face. This has been a day. Worst. Day. Ever.

I strip off my bloody clothes and ball them up in the corner of the bathroom. I take a washcloth and do my best to take a sink bath, washing away the dried blood on my body. Then, I put on a fluffy robe and go back into the room.

Kate and Justin have returned to their movie. Kate meets my eye as I make my way to my bed.

"Just ignore me," I tell her. "I'm going to lie down and read."

"Do you mind keeping it down?" Justin finally speaks.

I ball my hands into fists but don't respond. Forget that dude. I put on my headphones and just sit there, staring at the ceiling.

After a minute, I glance over at Justin and Kate. I guess the movie is over now, or maybe they decided it sucked because now Kate is crying on Justin's shoulder. He's patting her on the back. When he sees me looking, he rolls his eyes then looks at Kate and holds her chin up. Kate's red eyes meet Justin's gaze, and they both smile at one another. *Ugh, gross.* I go back to staring at the ceiling and listening to my headphones.

A few minutes later, Justin gets up to leave, and he and Kate spend ages saying goodnight at the door. *Why won't he just leave already?* I think sourly. Justin finally gives Kate one last kiss and then vanishes.

Kate shuts the door and twirls. "Scarlet," she says. "I have had *the* best night!" She twirls again, and I begin to take off my headphones to tell her about the shower disaster. She twirls her way past my bed and pushes the bathroom door open.

Then, I hear her scream.

"I told you not to go into the bathroom, didn't I?" I exclaim. "But I suppose you weren't paying attention since Justin probably was taking over all your thoughts, huh?"

"What? That's not true! You just ran in and told me not to go into the bathroom! I thought you had been hallucinating and spilled juice on yourself or something! I didn't know the blood was seeping in through the vent!" Kate yells at me.

I glare at her for a moment, but then something fuzzy niggles my brain. I never mentioned anything about the vent pipe to her, and the scene in our shower looks more like a body exploded in there, mostly from my cleaning attempts. How did she know about that? Did Justin pull her in on his sick plot? An uncomfortable silence stretches between us.

"What do you know about that blood in our shower?"

"I overheard Headmaster Jeong talking about it. All I know is that it's there," Kate answers.

I know she is lying. Her story just changed.

She grabs her robe and heads back into our bedroom. I follow her and get into bed myself, upset that my friend is keeping a secret from me but also relieved to put an end to this awful, awful day. I choose not to tell her that the body was discovered and the school is investigating as we speak.

When I wake up the next morning, I am astonished. Normally, I am the one to drag Kate out of bed, but today, she is already dressed and ready before me.

"Why are you up so early? Is there an event or something?" I ask her groggily, rubbing the sleep out of my eyes.

"No, I am just so energized!" Kate exclaims as though she's had ten cups of coffee.

"Right," I say. "Real funny, Kate. This is the first time you've gotten up and ready before me. What's going on with you?" My mind drifts back to the shower incident.

"Okay, Scarlet," Kate says, looking at me. There's a strange gleam in her eye that I've never seen before. "If you really want to know . . ." Kate steps toward me.

And then, everything goes black.

CHAPTER FOUR
A FRIEND'S BETRAYAL

RYAN

The bell for class rings, and I scramble through the door just before the sound finishes echoing in the halls. I quickly wind my way through the desks and take my seat, ready for a lesson in our Health and Wellness unit. At this academy, punctuality is regarded as one of our core tenets of discipline, and being late for class is not tolerated. Normally, I would never have even cut it this close, but after my conversation with Scarlet last night—well, let's just say I didn't sleep very well. All of my morning classes have been a blur, and I feel like a zombie, trudging through the motions mechanically.

With all the words left unsaid between us, I was counting on Scarlet to read between the lines and just trust me, but I have no idea what is going on in her head. My mind is already on our meeting later today. A bad sign when I need all of my concentration for my courses, especially since I already mentally blew off my morning classes. Oh well. I will get Justin to catch me up on those. Meeting with Scarlet in—I check my watch—thirty minutes is more important. In fact, she's in this class, too, and I'm eager to see if she's as distracted and unfocused as I am.

I shake my curls out of my eyes, and I look around the classroom at the rest of the Final Four, but one face, one blonde ponytail, is conspicuously absent.

Scarlet. Where is she? She's always present and punctual. After all, she didn't make it to the Final Four for nothing. Maybe I've been on her mind too?

"Today we will be learning how to stave off hunger," Instructor Sanchez, our health and wellness teacher, begins by way of introduction. My stomach gives a loud grumble, and I make a face. Yep. I for sure could have used a full night's rest and a protein-packed breakfast for this day.

"Preventing the effects of hunger from taking a mental toll on you is an important skill to develop in your careers as capturers," Instructor Sanchez goes on, her dark eyes glaring at us as if daring us to contradict her. We scribble down notes as she speaks. I glance over to Kate and try to catch her eye, but she is resolutely focused on her notetaking.

"Oftentimes on missions, you will not have the time, or the resources, to eat three meals a day. In this lesson, we will learn how to preserve your energy and stamina to stave off your hunger." Instructor Sanchez turns to begin writing on the blackboard, her sleek black hair gleaming under the fluorescent lights.

"Kate!" I hiss. "Kate!"

Kate finally looks up from her notes and glares at me. "What?" she says.

"Where's Scarlet?" I ask impatiently, leaning closer to her.

Kate's eyes rove over her notes for a moment before she answers me. "She's out sick."

"I thought we were prohibited from skipping class!" I say, unintentionally raising my voice. I wince as Instructor Sanchez whirls around.

"Mr. Pentaquese," Instructor Sanchez says in a tone that spells trouble for me. *Uh-oh.* "Thank you for the reminder, but you seem to have forgotten that you are also prohibited from talking out of turn and interrupting my lesson." She gives me a stern frown, and I shrink back in my chair. Instructor Sanchez teaches us combat as well, and I have seen what she can do with nothing but her fists. The last thing I want is to get on her wrong side.

"Yes, Instructor Sanchez," I reply meekly and do my best to look attentive, a portrait of the model student she knows me to be.

Instructor Sanchez narrows her eyes at me then begins talking about hunger and the brain's chemical signals. I know that each lesson here is important, and I know that not paying attention will bite me later, but try as I might, I cannot stay focused. Instructor Sanchez rambles on about ghrelin and the hypothalamus, her sentences punctuated by the sounds of scratching pencils.

Scarlet is probably fine, I tell myself. She probably just caught a bug or a cold, and the timing is coincidental. Probably nothing for me to be paranoid about.

I slump lower into my desk and stare at my notes before my gaze drifts back over to Kate. She is still focused on her notes and the lesson as though Instructor Sanchez's words are the most riveting she has ever heard. Odd for Kate. But maybe she's taking good notes for Scarlet for her to go over when she's feeling better.

Scritch, scritch, scritch.

The sound of everyone's pencils scratching out notes blends in with the ticking clock on the wall of the classroom. Maybe Scarlet will show up at the locker room for our meeting anyway. I mean, I know Scarlet, and I've seen how tough she is during our combat classes. You don't get to be in the Final Four by letting something like the sniffles keep you down. That's it. I've decided.

I shove my hand into the air. "Instructor Sanchez, may I use the restroom?" I ask abruptly.

"Fine, go," Instructor Sanchez responds, turning back to the blackboard and her lesson. My stomach gives another loud rumble—from hunger or nerves, I'm not quite sure. As quietly and quickly as I can, I stuff my notebook and pen into my backpack.

"What are you doing?" Kate mutters to me out of the counter of her mouth.

"Later," I whisper to her. I weave back out of the classroom into the empty hallway, ignoring the stares of my curious classmates and Kate's glare, which even at a distance, I can feel boring into the back of my head.

It's close to 2:30 now, the time when Scarlet and I are supposed to meet. I set off toward the locker room in a jog, berating myself for not just telling her everything yesterday. What if I scared her off?

As I get closer to the locker room, I peek around the corner to check if the coast is clear. No one is there. I creep toward the door and slink inside. Thankfully, it's empty. I tiptoe down the rows of lockers just to double-check. Yes, empty. I exhale and sit down on a bench near the door, resting my backpack on the floor. I'm a few minutes early, but Scarlet should be here any minute now. *If she comes.* If she trusts me enough to talk to me. My thoughts pick up again, mini tornados swirling in my mind, as I try to figure out how to tell her everything. Will she believe me? My leg jiggles nervously as I keep one eye on the door and the other on my watch, the second hand ticking by at a glacial speed. At 2:30, both my eyes are fixed on the door, and my body is frozen in anticipation. It's time. Scarlet should be here. But she hasn't shown.

By 2:35, my nervous knee-jiggling has picked up again, and by 2:40, I've got one eye back on my watch.

Maybe Scarlet really is sick, like Kate said. Maybe it wasn't just an excuse to avoid me. My leg-jiggling stops. Well, then, I guess I'm going to her dorm room to check. I toss my backpack over my shoulder and peer out the door of the locker room.

Thank goodness the halls are empty, and the passes for the Final Four between the boys' dorms and the girls' dorms are more relaxed. I reach Scarlet's door without running into a soul. I take a deep breath and knock softly. No answer.

"Scarlet?" I call quietly. "Scarlet, it's me. Are you there?" Still no answer. "I'm coming in."

I walk into her dorm room and glance around. Scarlet and Kate keep their dorm room pretty tidy, and my stomach twists guiltily at the thought of the piles of dirty laundry in my own dorm room. The books along the wall are neatly lined up on the shelves. Their desks are both mostly empty save for a notebook or two, likely last night's homework. Dim sunlight filters in through a crack in their curtains. "Scarlet?" I call tentatively.

Then I see her. She's lying on the floor, a small pool of blood around her head. "What happened? Scarlet!" I start toward her to see if she's okay, but I catch myself, my new training already kicking in, like a reflex. If this is a crime scene, I don't want to contaminate anything or mess up any evidence. Whoever did this needs to pay. I reach out and touch Scarlet's wrist to feel for a pulse, keeping my body as far away as possible. *There!* It's weak, but it's there.

"Scarlet," I tell her unconscious body. "I'm going to get help. I will be right back." I'm not sure why I say it since she clearly can't hear me, but it feels important that she knows I'm not abandoning her, that I'm here for her.

I sprint back to Instructor Sanchez's classroom and hurtle through the door, skidding to a halt just before I crash into the back row of desks.

"Mr. Pentaquese!" Instructor Sanchez exclaims. "This is the second time you've interrupted my class!"

Panting, I make out, "Scarlet . . . she's—she's . . . Please, follow me!" Instructor Sanchez rolls her eyes, irritated that I have interrupted her lesson yet again, but she must sense the urgency in my voice and sees the seriousness on my face, so she dismisses our class.

"Lead the way, Mr. Pentaquese," she says, gesturing to me. Kate peers at me curiously over her shoulder.

"Ryan, what's going on?" Kate asks, jogging next to me as we head to their dorm. "Is something wrong?"

"Just—I can't . . . I will show you," I stammer.

In just a few minutes, we are back outside their dorm room. Kate throws me a questioning glance as Instructor Sanchez slowly steps inside and gasps, her eyes dropping to the floor, to Scarlet's body. In a way, I'm relieved. For a moment I thought I had imagined everything, that this was all just a bad dream.

Instructor Sanchez puts her hand over Scarlet's heart.

"Still beating," she pronounces. "We need to take her to the nurse to find out what has happened." She whips out a phone from her pocket and presumably dials the nurse, yapping orders rapid-fire.

"Ryan," Kate says, looking seriously at me. "What happened here?"

I swallow, unable to tear my gaze away from Scarlet's prone body. Her blonde ponytail presents a cruel contrast to the dark blood around her head.

"I—I don't know," I whisper. "I just found her like this." I can't help but be struck by the timing. Does this have something to do with the fact that she was supposed to meet with me? Or with the information that I was supposed to give to her today in the locker room? Are they connected? I chew on my bottom lip. Oh, man. What if I'm responsible for this?

"Why were you in my dorm room?" Kate asks me. I tear my eyes away from Scarlet to meet Kate's gaze. She looks angry. Does she think I did this?

"I wanted to check on her. You said she was sick, and I . . . I just wanted to make sure she was okay," I say, avoiding the full truth.

Just then the nurse arrives, which cuts through the frosty tension building between Kate and me. She and Instructor Sanchez secure a brace around Scarlet's neck and carefully lift her onto a stretcher to take her to the medical wing.

"You can come with us if you want," Instructor Sanchez says, her eyes softening as she looks at Kate and me. "She's your friend. It might be good for you to be there when she wakes up."

I'm still completely shocked by finding Scarlet's body this way—with her blood on the floor—to even register Instructor Sanchez's compassion. I nod mutely and follow her and the nurse, Kate at my side.

When we arrive at the emergency wing of our school, the nurse gently lays Scarlet down on a cot. She pushes Scarlet's hair back and examines the cut on her head with a keen eye, muttering to herself. Under the fluorescent lights of the medical wing, Scarlet's blood gleams red and wet across her pale face. The nurse takes a cloth and gently wipes the blood off of Scarlet's face and head, but more oozes out from the wound after it's cleaned.

I swallow thickly. I've never been great around blood, and there's so much of it. Kate sinks down to a bench near the foot of the cot.

The nurse takes a small tube from a tray nearby and rubs an ointment on the cut on Scarlet's head. The ointment goes on thick and gloopy, turning pink as it mixes with her blood. Taking a thick piece of gauze from the tray, the nurse places it over Scarlet's forehead and tapes it over the cut. Next, she forces one of Scarlet's eyes open and shines a penlight into it, and then does the same to the other eye.

Kate and I watch silently, not looking at one another, our own eyes fixed on the nurse as she ministers to Scarlet.

"Looks like her cut is shallow, but head wounds bleed a lot," the nurse says to Instructor Sanchez or maybe to us—I'm not sure. I don't really care. "She might have a concussion, but she will be okay."

The nurse stands up from her stool and motions for Instructor Sanchez to follow her into her office, presumably to talk to her in private about Scarlet's condition or how this possibly could have happened. I am paralyzed, stuck right where I'm standing, as if my feet have sprouted roots that go deep into the floor. Although I don't feel strong and sturdy like a tree. My head feels light and hazy and my knees like they might buckle and give out on me at any moment. How did this happen? And am I responsible?

I narrow my eyes and try to focus. If the information I was about to give Scarlet was connected to her accident, who would know? Who else knew we were meeting? Or about what I was going to tell her? My gut clenches as I swallow back the bile building in my stomach. Out of the corner of my eye, I see something move. I assume it's Instructor Sanchez and the nurse returning.

But just then, Scarlet's eyes shoot wide open, and she snaps up from her hospital cot, sitting ramrod straight. I jump back, startled by the sudden movement, adrenaline coursing through my veins.

"Scarlet!" I cry, both alarmed and relieved.

Her eyes are unfocused, and she gingerly reaches up to touch the wound on her head. She flinches and draws her hand away. She sees me standing there, and her eyes click into focus.

"Ryan," she says hoarsely and immediately starts blurting out what happened to her. When she finishes explaining, I turn to look at Kate.

But Kate is gone.

Gone as if she had never been there in the first place. There is no sign of her; although I could have sworn she had just been standing there. *When did she slip out?*

My eyes meet Scarlet's.

"I should get Instructor Sanchez," I say. "She needs to know all this. If Kate is behind this . . ." I trail off, noticing that Scarlet's gaze is fixed upon a single slice of fabric on the bench where Kate had been sitting. I look at Scarlet intently then reach for the cloth and pass it to her, looking down at it as she holds it in her hands.

Her hands run over the fabric as if examining it by touch. She flips it over and there is something written on it.

53W70

"What does it mean?" I ask Scarlet as I finish reading it. "53W70? Is it some sort of code?"

But rather than answer me, Scarlet leaps out of her bed and bolts out the door.

"Scarlet!" I shout, and Instructor Sanchez and the nurse come barreling out of the nurse's office.

"Scarlet! Where are you going? The exit's that—" I call out, but she cuts me off.

"I'm not going there," Scarlet shoots back, nodding her head once while glancing back at us.

"Then where?" I ask, as I jog toward her, Instructor Sanchez and the nurse behind me.

"Just shut up and follow me!" Scarlet yells urgently. The three of us dash after her, a tense silence hanging in the air, broken only by our panting breaths as we sprint, full-out.

Scarlet suddenly stops running and she turns to us. We skid to a halt in front of her.

Instructor Sanchez, the nurse, and I all stare back at Scarlet, waiting for an explanation. I glance around us. We are currently standing inside a hallway outside a door that looks to lead down to the basement. What is going on?

"The basement," Scarlet says slowly. "Where the body was." She puts her head down and trembles.

"Scarlet," I say tentatively. "I know you just got hurt and all, so maybe it's not the best time for us to be running around and going to the . . . the basement."

The nurse comes up behind Scarlet and rubs her back in soothing circles. "Scarlet, you have a concussion," the nurse tells her. "You need to take it easy."

Instructor Sanchez looks at Scarlet curiously. "The basement?" she pushes Scarlet. "Where the body was?"

Scarlet looks up at her as sweat drips down her face. "Yes," Scarlet breathes. And something shifts behind Scarlet's eyes. I have no idea what secrets the basement holds or what body she is talking about, but the fear on Scarlet's face is plain.

She's terrified.

Chapter Five
Escape

KATE

"She has a concussion, but she will be okay," the nurse pronounces after examining Scarlet. She and Instructor Sanchez step out of the room, leaving me alone with Ryan and Scarlet.

My blood is cold, and a dull thud resounds in my ears as I gaze at Scarlet's limp body on the cot. The fluorescent lights of the medical wing cast shadows on her face, making her look skeleton-like. Her cheeks appear sunken beneath the dark half-moons under her eyes, and I shiver—I can't help it.

To distract myself, I look over at Ryan who is staring down at Scarlet, completely transfixed. His golden skin has lost its glow. His face is pallid, his eyes bloodshot and strained. *Hmm, maybe he is more into her than I initially thought.*

I glance down at my watch. I expect her to be out cold for at least a few more hours. I flex my wrist, remembering how the metal pole I had grabbed from under my pillow felt in my hand before I bludgeoned Scarlet across the head, confusion on her face as I approached and swung. She didn't even try to protect herself. Honestly, I expected more of a fight from her.

But now that I see her lying unconscious here, my skin prickles uncomfortably, and I rub my arms. At first, I was simply playing the role of concerned roommate and friend, but the longer I sit here in the medical wing, the less this becomes just a role. My eyes drift back to her. She just looks so helpless.

But eventually, she is going to wake up, and I need to be out of here when she does. Panic rushes up inside me at the thought. What will happen to me when Scarlet wakes up? How much will she remember? If she knows it's me . . . well, it's her word against mine, but seeing as how Scarlet has a giant gash on her head, that seems to be a point in her favor. What I need is a distraction, something to throw them off and buy me time to get out of here.

I glance back at Ryan who seems to have forgotten I'm even there. I tear off a piece of my jacket. The ripping sound sounds loud to me, and I flinch. Luckily, Ryan doesn't move. I reach up and take out one of my earrings, and, using the pointed tip, I scratch a message into the rough leather.

53W70

Although the numbers in my coded message look like an area code, they are the numerical values of letters that translate to a location: SEWER.

I quietly place the ripped fabric on the bench next to me and stand up. The panic that had threatened to overwhelm me has been replaced by resolve. I know what I need to do now. Quickly, I leave the medical wing. Ryan doesn't even seem to notice as I retreat. So much the better.

Scarlet will wake up soon and see the clue I left for her. Knowing Scarlet, she will most likely not pay attention to the details. I'm betting on her running out the front door instead. I slow down my pace when I realize this.

I make my way into the basement and hurry toward the trap doors I know lead to the sewer system. The underground system runs for miles and connects our school with the city and some small towns nearby. I tread slowly down into the chambers of the sewers. I wrap my scarf around my face to protect against the mildew and the moldy air. No matter how many times I've been down here, I cannot ever quite get past the thickness of the odors that permeate through the air, smells of dirt, urine, and stale water.

It's so still down here, peaceful even. The only sounds are the pinging droplets of water that fall from the pipes. The soft pings echo through the empty tunnels, and the sound is reassuring. I am alone.

I feel cold inside. Not because of the chilly atmosphere of the sewers. No, my chill runs down into my bones, into my very soul. *What have I done? What have I become?* My head and my heart seem to be at war with one another, one part screaming at me that I did what was necessary and the other yelling back that I am supposed to be her friend.

I shush that second voice and cram it into a box hidden deep inside me. It's too late for that now. I have already chosen my path forward. What's done is done, and if Scarlet has any sense, she will do well to forget all about me.

I kick a rock, and it clangs loudly through the quiet tunnels. I freeze, holding my breath to make sure I'm still hidden, still undiscovered. All is silent save for the steady *drip, drip, drip* of condensation falling. I let out a breath of relief through the scarf wrapped around my face and take another step forward. Then I hear it.

Voices echoing from behind me, coming from the sewer entrance.

"Why would Kate do such a thing?" I hear Ryan's voice bounce through the tunnels.

"Why do people eat? Breathe? Sleep?" another voice retorts. "Because we have that option! If you really wanted to, you could just stop breathing!" I strain my ears. That sounds like Instructor Sanchez.

"But—"

"You can also stop talking. You have that option too."

Definitely Instructor Sanchez.

I break into a steady jog. I did not expect them to come down here right off the bat. Did Scarlet really figure out my code that quickly? Perhaps I underestimate her. I pick up my pace and start running through the tunnels, my dangly earrings bouncing against my cheeks—wait, no. Earring. singular. As I continue to run, I reach up and check, just to be sure. It's bare. My earring is gone.

"Crap," I curse under my breath as I realize the magnitude of my mistake. I pump my legs harder and will myself to go faster, faster. I pull the scarf down from my mouth and gulp in a lungful of thick air as I speed down the tunnels.

My foot sinks into a deep puddle of sewer water I failed to notice, and I trip, falling spectacularly as I sprawl out on the damp floor of the tunnel. The wind is knocked out of me when I hit the ground. I quickly pull myself up, fighting and gasping to regain my breath, and take off again. My footsteps squelch loudly with every other step.

Great, I'm leaving wet footprints behind!

I skid to a halt and lift my soaked shoe off of the ground. I pull at it—it's completely drenched—and throw it as hard as I can ahead of me. I hear it land with a thud. Instead of taking off after it, I climb up the pipes. With only one shoe now and only one earring, this escape is not going quite how I intended it.

Up, up, up the pipes I go until I get to the top of the sewer channel. Up here in the shadows, I am hidden and have a bird's-eye view of the scene below me. The nearest grate is thirty feet behind me down the tunnel, a dim light filtering through down to the ground below. I sit silently at my perch and watch, waiting.

"Guys, look! Kate's earring! She must be down here! It has to be her!" I hear someone shout, their voice echoing loudly through the sewers. *Those idiots should keep quiet if they are trying to sneak up on me and catch me unaware,* I say to myself. They give themselves away with every echoing word.

My mind races faster than my feet did as I try to put together a plan. I thought I would have more time to reach a hideout and escape. Clearly, I was wrong.

I hear their steps before I see them. Their shuffling footfalls, their labored breathing through the thick sewer air, and their echoing voices. Soon, they step into the filtered light from the grate, and I tense, barely allowing myself to breathe. They should spot my wet footprints anytime now.

"Footprints, look!" Ryan exclaims, pointing down. *Right on cue.*

"They're still wet. She must have been here recently," Instructor Sanchez says. Soon, they should find my discarded shoe as well.

Scarlet wanders into the light behind Ryan and Instructor Sanchez. She looks particularly worse for the wear as she trudges along the dark sewer—even paler than usual, practically glowing in the dim tunnels. Her blonde hair, streaked red with blood, is pulled back in her usual ponytail, and her hair frizzes around her head like a messed-up halo.

"We can find her if we follow the footsteps," Ryan says, an upward lilt of excitement in his voice.

"Ryan," Scarlet snaps. "You do not need to point out every single detail. We all have these things called eyes."

I smirk, imagining a red flush creeping up Ryan's neck, into his face, and spreading across his cheeks.

As they approach the ground beneath my hiding spot, I will my body to shrink into the shadows high above their heads. I wrap my scarf around my mouth to stifle any sounds, but I still don't want to risk it. I hold my breath.

They pass beneath me, their eyes glued to the ground and my wet footprints. Luckily, no one has the sense to look up. I'm not off the hook yet, though. I can't let myself relax or feel any sense of ease until I'm confident they are gone.

"The tracks either dry up or stop here," the nurse says, looking around. She hunches down as if getting closer to the dirty ground will allow her to see the tracks more clearly, and I have to make an effort to suppress my laughter. She bends down even further, her hands on her knees, her backside swinging in the air, and I bite my lip. The absurd visual is hysterical.

"Hey, what's that?" Ryan calls back to them from up the tunnel. "It's a—is that a shoe?" He sounds unsure of himself. Come on, Ryan, it's not that hard to identify a shoe. Honestly, what does Scarlet see in him? Could he be any more naïve? How did he make Final Four?

Ryan comes back to the others with my shoe in his hand. He shows it to Scarlet. "Is this Kate's?" he asks her gently, as if afraid she will bite his head off again.

"Yes," Scarlet answers without touching the filthy shoe. I'm also a little grossed out by the fact that Ryan so readily picked up my nasty sewer shoe, to be honest, even if it was on my own foot not too long ago.

"I don't see any more footprints, though, do you?" Ryan asks the group. They must be shaking their heads—I can't tell in the dim light—because then Ryan says, "Well, now we have to just guess where she went from here."

"Maybe down this way?" the nurse suggests, pointing to a side tunnel.

I've thrown them off my trail. My plan worked. I finally let myself exhale a sigh of relief.

Below me, Scarlet suddenly looks around, her head whipping left and right. *Oh, no, did she hear me?* Adrenaline courses through my body like electricity in my veins. And then Scarlet looks up into the pipes.

"Must have been my imagination," she says to herself quietly.

Her gaze leaves the spot right where I had been perched only a moment before.

"Let's go down this way," Instructor Sanchez calls, and the motley group sets off down the side tunnel.

I am pressed against a wall, still hidden in the shadows, feeling grateful for the hours and hours of training with Instructor Sanchez that have made my body so quick and so nimble. That was close. I wait a few minutes after they are gone before I continue running again, not sure exactly where

I am going, just racing in the direction opposite the one Scarlet went in.

I don't know how long I run. My watch tells me it's late into the night, but I still keep running and running, one sneakered foot and one bare foot. My stocking foot pounding the ground of the tunnels, causing the bones in that leg to ache. I hadn't realized how much protection my shoe offered me, and rocks and other debris poke painfully into my foot as I start to half limp, half run.

I climb up a sewer ladder and push myself out. Gratefully, I pull the scarf down from my face and neck and breathe in the fresh air. My desperate lungs greedily take in large gulps. A slight breeze blows my damp hair away from my face, the wind cools my sweaty neck. I carefully replace the manhole cover back over the sewer entrance and survey my surroundings.

I appear to be in the middle of nowhere. The land around me is dry and barren with only a few sparse trees in the distance surrounding a small lake. There is no light apart from the twinkling stars above me and the half-moon hanging in the sky. From what I can tell, I am miles away from any city. *Perfect.*

I roll my shoulders and start walking around. Crickets chirp around me, and an owl hoots, but blessedly, all else is quiet and still. I walk in peace for a while, relieved to be outside after hours in the sewer tunnels. I wonder how long Scarlet will look for me, how long it will be before they give up their search. I also wonder what Scarlet has told them. It will not take long for word to spread; our school is not that big. What will my classmates think when they find out? What will Justin think? My stomach clenches, and I stop walking.

I pull off my backpack. I had planned for this, so in addition to my school things, my extra-large backpack contains a few bottles of water, dried fruit, jerky and hard cheese, a pocketknife, a handgun with multiple rounds of ammunition, a Taser, a sleeping bag, and a small tent. It's remarkable that no one noticed how bulky my backpack was today.

It seems like long ago that I was sitting in class, almost as if that setting was a whole other world. It might as well be for what my life will look like going forward. I know I need to say goodbye to the comforts of regular meals from the cafeteria, a warm bed in a cozy dorm room, and worries that only ever last as long as a school test. My problems are much larger than that now. It seems ludicrous to me that just the other night, I was snuggled in bed, kissing Justin while we watched a movie we'd seen a hundred times already. It strikes me as something very young, very teenaged.

I am still wearing my school uniform: a now-torn black jumper emblazoned with our school crest. It seems so at odds with how old I feel right now. Schoolgirl Kate was a different age with a different life. I eye the crest on the chest of my blazer and rip it off. I stare at it for a moment, taking in how definite it feels now that I am done with that life, done with school. The crest feels heavier than it should in my hand. I kneel down on the ground and scoop aside some dirt with my hands, creating a small hole, a shallow grave. I place the crest at the bottom and sweep the pile of dirt back over it. So long, schoolgirl Kate. Rest in peace.

I then walk over to a grove of trees and start setting up a campsite.

Though exhausted, I feel completely calm. I have been trained for this. In our survival class at school, we were taught how to prepare for and cope with situations like this. First step: find a clean water source. The stream bubbling nearby should be good for that when my water bottles run low. Second step: set up your camp. We are each given a tracker that we can activate, like a digital flare gun, so the headmasters can trace our location and help us return to school.

But I will never set foot in that school again.

I shuffle through my backpack and pull out the tracker. It's small—smaller than the size of my palm. Methodically, I place it on a large rock. I grab another rock in my hand and smash it several times. It cracks open, and I am pleased to see that the electronic components inside are broken. No one will be tracking me.

I pull out my tent and get to work setting it up. It's small and far from luxurious, but it provides shelter and some protection. My stomach rumbles loudly, and I remember it's been a while since I've had anything to eat or drink. I need to keep up my energy if this is going to work. I reach for a water bottle and some dried fruit.

Just then, I hear a crackle in the bushes near my tent. I freeze, my water bottle halfway to my lips, and listen hard.

I slowly reach into my bag and pull out my gun, clicking the safety off.

Another crack sounds, this time even closer.

"Who is there? Show yourself or I will shoot!" I say, projecting as much confidence into my voice as I can. The truth is, even though I'm alarmed, I am not scared. I must be miles away from the school and the chances that a casual civilian could take me down are slim.

A figure dressed in all black slowly emerges from the bushes, a hood covering his face. I sigh in relief as he pulls his hoodie down, and I spy the face of one of my colleagues.

"I hate you! Why did you scare me like that?" I say, shoving him.

But he does not return my jest. His eyes are cold and his face fearful.

"Run. As far as you can. They're coming back. They have the government on their side now. Run!"

Chapter Six
A Suspect Among Us

Ryan

It was only a few weeks ago that my parents enrolled me in this school called Captures. Only a few weeks, but it feels like so much longer. Time seems to run together at this school, each day a repetition of the same litany of physical training, mental training, and pure exhaustion. Each day, a set of new challenges tests us and pushes us to the brink of what we're capable of, the edge of what our bodies can handle, and the limit of how far our minds can stretch without breaking.

Jack is my older brother who's been at this school for a few years now, and although we've never been the tightest, I had hoped that being at Captures would pull us closer together. In the last few years, our family has been through some really difficult times—like more tragedy than what regular folks go through. You think you've got problems at home, but I swear, it's nothing compared to the problems we've had, the things we've gone through. Talk about deep, dark family secrets.

Anyway, I was hopeful that enrolling at Captures was our chance: it was supposed to be an opportunity for us to talk through some of our family baggage and make our way through it together, as brothers. With our parents largely absent these days, sometimes, it feels like we're all each other has left.

When I took the entrance exam and applied to Captures, I easily mastered every physical and mental challenge they threw at me. Because of this, the school administrators placed me in the elite training class—the Final Four. I was relieved because Jack was an elite fighter himself, and I didn't want to let him down. He's my brother after all, and I wanted him to be proud of me. Although Jack and I haven't always gotten along, and our relationship was pretty strained when he left for school—to say the least—I was still rooting for him. Sure, he had always been closer to our sister, Siffrin. I didn't mind. I mean, maybe I was a little jealous of how close she and Jack were, even though I realize that's stupid and petty of me. But really, I just wanted what was best for my bro.

And so, a sense of pride had warmed my chest when I heard of how he'd succeeded at this brutal school. Having taken the challenges myself, I now knew how grueling they were. I now knew how hard this school was. Maybe now we could start working through some of our family secrets together. That was the plan.

But I realize today, my plan is more like a pie-in-the-sky fantasy.

Yesterday, Jack pulled me over and said we needed to talk. He looked worried and completely out-of-sorts. He told me that when you've been enrolled in a school that teaches you to be alert, to watch for weaknesses, you start to see them everywhere. He said that he had come to know the people here: their personalities, their secrets, and their agendas. And what he realized is that some people at this school are not who they say they are.

Like Kate.

"I'm not sure if this school knows who Kate truly is, but I don't know what kind of game they are playing if they do. If they'd known what Kate had done, I can't imagine why they would recruit her for Captures rather than stick her in a jail cell or some juvenile detention center somewhere. Because Kate does not deserve her freedom. Not after what she's done," Jack spat out frantically.

The story Jack told me then was heartbreaking and infuriating at the same time. Kate is a murderer.

Years ago, before Jack really figured out this school, before he got a feeling of who each person—each student and teacher—our aunt died. Now, Jack was telling me that she wasn't just killed as part of a robbery gone awry, as the police report said. She was murdered, and Jack had seen it happen.

It was a clean kill, he said, not as messy as you might expect a murder to be. Very minimal blood, very little gore. The whole scene was so clinical that you'd think it was nothing more than a medical procedure or something—except that our aunt would never wake up. The killers were professionals, that much was clear to him. One gunshot and it was over. Aunt Loretta never saw it coming.

Jack was on a school break from Captures, so he was spending time at home with our family. Jack and I had just had a fight, and while I thought he ran off to Siffrin's, he had gone over to our aunt's apartment to stay the night and spend some time away from us to cool off. I don't even remember what our fight was about, and it seems so silly that this detail slips my memory, and that bothers me now. Even though I can't remember the fight clearly, I regret it deeply. If it weren't for that fight, everything might have been different. Our family might still be together, and our aunt might still be alive. And I can't remember it.

Aunt Loretta and Jack had a late dinner together, and she talked him down from his anger. She was good at that, always encouraging us to try to see things from other points of view and look at situations from all angles, a lesson that has stuck with us. She taught us the power of observation and how sometimes, it is better to watch, assess, calculate, and plan before you act. Another lesson that's stuck with me.

Jack told me that everything felt so normal that night, so calm. She was in a pair of sweats and a T-shirt and making some hot cocoa for them to wind down for the night. I can almost see the small and cozy apartment and hear our auntie's voice when Jack was describing the events of that evening. Aunt Loretta liked her hot chocolate with whole milk. "If you're going to make hot cocoa," she would always say, "you gotta use whole milk to get that full richness." I didn't really know what she was talking about, what "that full richness" was. Whole milk, skim milk, 2%—it all tasted the same to me once you stirred in the hot chocolate mix.

The milk was heated on the stovetop, and Aunt Loretta gently stirred in the chocolate mix and poured it into their two mugs. Then her face froze and her whole body stiffened. "Jack," she said, all levity gone from her tone. And then Aunt Loretta was pushing my brother into a coat closet, shoving him behind a fake wall hidden in there.

What's crazy is that Jack wasn't confused or bothered by the fact of the wall, he said. No, the thing that stuck out to him the most, he later realized, was that Aunt Loretta had a ton of winter coats in her coat closet. *What does one woman, who lives alone, need all these winter coats for?* he had wondered. It's strange how your mind jumps to ordinary curiosities like that, as if his brain couldn't handle questioning the fake wall right then or why Aunt Loretta was hiding him behind it. It was the stupid coats that had preoccupied him.

To this day, he is not sure why our aunt was targeted. She worked a government job, but I don't know the specifics, and our aunt will never tell us given that she's in a cold grave somewhere.

Jack's face was laced with tears as he told me about the peephole in the fake wall and how he had peered through it, between the winter coats and through the slats in the closet door. What was going on? Was this some whack dream? Aunt Loretta stood calmly facing the door, her hands hanging loosely by her sides as if she was waiting for a guest to come over. Confusion swirled in Jack's head as he watched, waiting for the door to open, for Aunt Loretta to greet her mysterious late-night visitor. He recalled that, somehow, he was still holding his mug of hot chocolate.

But the door never opened. After a few seconds, there was a soft *pop!* and Aunt Loretta crumbled to the floor. Rather than fear, my brother only felt confusion. Surely this was a bad dream. He thought he was going to wake up, safe in bed. Or maybe this was some psychological test at Captures. That must be it; it had to be a test. To see how he would cope with stress or something. To push his mind to the brink before reeling him back.

As Jack told his story, I kept inhaling deeply, trying to clear away the pain and shock. It seemed like the warm scent of my aunt's hot chocolate filled my nose along with something tangy that smelled like iron. The sensation was so real that I had to shake my head to help me return to reality and concentrate.

From his vantage point in the closet, Jack only had a small window into what was happening in the apartment. All he could see was the hallway that led from the entryway.

A shadowy figure came into view from the direction of the kitchen. The figure wore all black with gloves covering his hands, and a mask obscured his face.

"Check the apartment," the figure said tersely, and my brother watched him put a gun with a silencer into his belt.

This is when it got real for Jack. A gun! This man had a gun! His addled brain started putting the pieces together, and when the realization hit him like a freight train, he stuffed his fist into his mouth to keep from screaming, from sobbing out loud. Hot tears rolled silently down my brother's cheeks. Jack said that his hand, which was clutching his mug, started shaking, and lukewarm liquid sloshed over his knuckles.

This wasn't a dream, and this wasn't a test.

This was real.

Aunt Loretta was dead, and Jack knew it. He knew this man who had shot and killed her was a professional and would leave nothing to chance. Aunt Loretta seemed to be expecting him, but she still never saw him coming. Bizarrely, Jack wondered how he had gotten into the apartment and what he had been doing in the kitchen.

"Bedroom and bathroom all clear," reported voice, one that sounded female.

"Check that closet," the man's voice back toward the kitchen.

Suddenly, light flooded the cl and the coats were shuffled through hidden behind the wall, that they wo

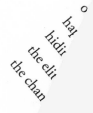

suspect it was a fake, he drew back and held his breath. From the peephole, Jack saw a girl's face, one not much younger than him. She had pushed her mask up and sweat dotted her forehead. Jack memorized her face and swore he would remember it until the day he died.

"All clear," the girl reported tonelessly.

Jack was the only eyewitness to my aunt's murder, and he never forgets a face.

My brother knew who she was . . . at the moment he saw her at Captures.

Kate. The girl who helped kill my aunt.

I had tried and failed to warn Scarlett that her BFF is actually a killer in disguise.

Like I said, our family's problems are not your run-of-the-mill family problems. And there's more.

Shortly after our aunt died, Siffrin went missing. Was she dead? Was she faking her death to hide from the same people who killed Aunt Loretta? We have no idea, but our family doesn't talk much about Siffrin or Aunt Loretta anymore. I suspect that Siffrin's disappearance, though, is one of the reasons why our parents pushed hard for me to join Jack at Captures. Now my parents have both of us out of the house and out of their hair while they continue trying to figure out what happened to Aunt Loretta and find where Siffrin might be going . . . if she's still alive, that is. And with two sons joining the school to become professional capturers—the greater chances these two mysteries will be solved.

So, yeah. You might say that the Pentaquese family has a lot going on and more than enough dark secrets to hide. One thing is for certain, though: with Aunt Loretta dead and Siffrin more than likely also dead, I've gotta watch out for my brother. I owe that to him.

Scarlett certainly doesn't know the secrets hidden in Kate's past, what's she's a part of. That's what I wanted to share with Scarlett when I asked her to meet me at the lockers. Maybe if I didn't wait, maybe if I told her that same night, none of this would have happened.

CHAPTER SEVEN

A CRIMINAL ON THE LOOSE

SCARLET

"Hey, what's that?" Ryan calls, his voice echoing through the tunnel. "It's a . . . is that a shoe?" A chorus of *shoe, shoe, shoe* resounds around us, each one pounding into my tender head. Maybe running into the sewer tunnels so soon wasn't such a good idea. Captures has trained us extensively on when to observe and when to act, but it's a balance I have always struggled with. Time is of the essence in this situation, I told my pounding head, and we have to act.

"Is this Kate's?" Ryan trots back down the tunnel to where I'm standing, clutching onto the shoe like it's a precious new-born baby. A smile lights up his whole face as he nears me, and it's strange to see him being so warm toward me given his coldness earlier when he wanted nothing to do with me. That confusion in and of itself makes my already woozy head spin harder.

Ryan hands me the filthy shoe, but I keep my hands to myself, leaving the shoe in his outstretched hand. "Yes," I say shortly, wrinkling my nose. If Kate's shoe is here, that means Kate must be—or at least had been—nearby. We are getting close.

"I don't see any more footprints, though, do you?" Ryan looks around, the shoe still extended. "Well, now we have to just guess where she went from here." He finally withdraws the shoe back to his side. That thing is nasty, and I don't even want to think of all the germs and who knows what else that Ryan is getting all over his hands by touching it. But dang, if this is where the trail goes cold, that doesn't bode well. We have to be close, though. Kate couldn't have gotten in these sewers with only one shoe.

A hand touches my elbow, and I practically jump out of my own shoes. It's just the nurse. I had forgotten she is with us, which doesn't seem like such a great sign for my concussed brain. "Maybe down this way?" the nurse suggests, pointing toward a tunnel.

My head throbs, and I shrug. Her guess is as good as any of ours at the moment. I close my eyes, trying to get ahold of myself, of everything that has happened today. Tears prick the corners of my eyes, and I squeeze them shut even harder as if I can push away the wetness by force. The pounding in my head is like a drumbeat, a rhythm of pain and betrayal, and a single tear leaks out.

How could Kate have done this?

How could anyone have done this? Kate is so much more to me than just a classmate and roommate. She is my confidant, my best friend. Kate is—was—like a sister to me. The one who I turned to for comfort when I was feeling down, and she was always there with a hug and chocolate. The one who celebrated my wins with dance parties in our dorm room and extra cookies smuggled out of the cafeteria. What happened?

Was it all an act? Was our friendship even real? Was her friendship part of her cover, part of the cloak she used to conceal her agenda?

And what was her agenda anyway? What did it have to do with me?

I inhale a deep breath, the smell of damp tunnel filling my nostrils, and I count to five. I tilt my head back and exhale, counting to five again, my eyes remaining firmly closed as I get a grip on my emotions. Another rebel tear leaks out. More deep breaths. *In, two, three, four, five. Out, two, three, four, five.*

Kate is not my best friend, that much is clear. My best friend never would have assaulted me and left me for dead. My best friend never would have run from me. If Kate is in some sort of trouble, surely there would have been signs.

Surely, she would have talked to me about it. We could have figured it out together. If someone had something on her, she could have told me, and we would have faced it together. We had no secrets from each other. I thought we told each other nearly everything, but I was wrong. So, so wrong. More tears fall slowly down my cheeks.

Suddenly, I hear a sigh. My eyes snap open, and I whip my head around looking for the source. Ryan and the nurse are up the tunnel some distance, Instructor Sanchez just behind them. The sound did not come from them.

I narrow my eyes, taking in my surroundings—the bleak expanse of the tunnel walls, the pipes running up them.

The pipes!

My eyes slowly sweep upward, following the path of the pipes. I take in every detail, every drop of condensation, every cobweb, every cockroach scuttling around, all the way up to the top.

Nothing.

There's nothing there. All is empty save for the roaches skittering along the walls.

"Must have been my imagination," I mutter to myself. I could have sworn I heard something. It was probably just my mind playing tricks on me, an aftereffect of my concussion. My brain wants Kate to give herself away, so that's what my ears heard. I pinch the bridge of my nose and try to ground myself back in the moment, and my head gives a particularly painful throb. I shouldn't have ever left the medical wing.

Why didn't I at least grab some painkillers before we ran down here on this fruitless mission? Maybe the nurse travels with pain relievers, I wonder dully.

Instructor Sanchez's voice interrupts my private pity party. "Let's go down this way," she says, indicating the tunnel the nurse pointed to a few minutes ago. I take a few steps before my woozy thoughts return to me.

It was stupid to have come down here. We have no idea where Kate went. All she left us with is her earring and her shoe. She's probably long gone by now, although a petty part of me grins savagely at the fact that she only has one shoe. I hope it slows her down and causes her discomfort. Maybe she will step on something sharp and be slowly consumed with tetanus or get bit by a rat or something while she's down here. But I know it's only a halfhearted wish.

As part of the Final Four, she has been trained to be the one who does the capturing, not the one who gets captured. We are instructed in the twin arts of avoiding detection and bringing in criminals, even under the worst conditions. Compared to what we've been trained to cope with, a missing shoe is nothing.

I have to accept the facts. We had our chance to catch her. We had a few moments where we might have been gaining on her, but she outran us. Outsmarted us. We blew it.

I blew it.

Our group walks silently down the tunnel together, our footsteps thudding dully on the ground, a tempo that pounds against my poor brain. I open my mouth to ask the nurse if she has anything then close it again. It was my own hot head and lack of foresight that pulled us down here with no plan. I deserve this pain. I can hold up for a bit longer.

Instead, I glance at Ryan. He's still holding Kate's shoe, our clue that she really had been down here, that she is running. His eyes are downcast, and his shoulders bow inward. He looks visibly deflated, and I can tell he's disappointed that the trail has gone cold, especially since it felt like we were so close for a second. A muscle twitches in his jaw as if he's clenching his teeth.

He must feel me looking at him because he glances over at me. Although his eyes are round and sad, like a puppy dog's, he forces a smile. I'm not sure if it's meant for me or for himself.

"We will get her," he says, and again, I wonder if he is speaking more to himself than to me. "She only has one shoe. She can't make it that far without help. Right?" How does he resemble a puppy so much right now? "Scarlet, I—" He looks down once more and swallows thickly, his Adam's apple bobbing in his throat. "Scarlet, I'm so sorry this happened to you. I'm so sorry that she hurt you. And she was with me . . . she was with me, and I didn't know."

He looks back up at me. There's a new fierceness in his dark eyes underneath his furrowed brows. He takes one of my hands in his, and despite the grime coating his palm, I don't pull back. His hand is warm and safe against mine, and

I absorb the comfort it brings me. For a moment, I don't feel my pounding head or my exhausted body. I only feel his hand in mine, the warmth that spreads through my fingers and up my arms, and my heart hums in peaceful content.

"I didn't know," Ryan whispers again, blinking back tears of his own. "And I'm so sorry. If I had known she had hurt you . . ." His voice cracks, and a tear falls from his watery eyes, sliding down his cheek. His eyes, now filled with tears—tears meant for me—sparkle in the dim light in the tunnels. My breath catches, and my heart hums louder. Sweet, sweet Ryan.

I squeeze his hand. "It's not your fault," I murmur. "Nobody saw this coming. I feel so stupid, and I'm kicking myself for not realizing something was wrong with her. But Ryan, look at me. Look at me." He holds my gaze, his dark eyes focused on mine. "There were no signs. Nobody had any idea. Kate pulled the wool over all of our eyes. This is not on you."

It feels strange that I, the one with the banged-up brain, whose head is bleeding, am the one offering words of comfort to him. But it also feels right, and I know that my words are true. No one could have predicted this. No one knew this might be coming. Even Instructor Sanchez seems shocked by the turn of events.

Still holding Ryan's hand, I look up ahead to where Instructor Sanchez and the nurse are strolling a few feet in front of us, talking in hushed tones and shining flashlights around the tunnel halfheartedly.

"If there's anything I can do to make this up to you—anything . . ." Ryan says earnestly, and his puppy-dog expression comes back.

"Thanks, Ryan. I appreciate that," I say, and he squeezes my hand gratefully. But I know that I will never take him up on his offer. This battle with Kate is personal now, and so much the better for him to stay safe and stay out of it. Who knows what Kate is capable of?

As we walk on, Instructor Sanchez kicks a rock angrily and lets out a curse in frustration. We've officially admitted defeat. We've lost the trail. I sigh.

After a few more minutes of walking, our flashlights roaming over the ground even as Ryan's hand never leaves mine, Instructor Sanchez tells us that we should head back to the school.

We trudge upward, no one speaking. I can't wait to fall into my bed with some painkillers and sleep this awful day off. I hope I will wake up and find out that this has been some kind of nightmare. That I will wake up nervously anticipating my meeting with Ryan in the locker room. What had seemed so important just last night, knowing why he was suddenly so cold to me, is trivial now. Maybe it's because he is walking alongside me, shooting me sideways glances, and his warm hand is in mine. Or maybe it's because my pulsing head cannot process any more emotions right now. But I can't summon the energy or the willpower to ask him about that, to ask what was so important yesterday that it warranted a secret locker-room meeting.

Night is beginning to fall as we approach the school. The lamps around the school have turned on, and a warm glow floods the ground. A few stars twinkle innocently above us.

"I do have one last idea," Instructor Sanchez tells us, as she pushes open the door to the school and directs us toward her office. "It's a long shot, but it's worth a try."

Ryan perks up at that, the idea there is any shot at all, no matter how unlikely, giving him a second round of energy and putting the wind back in his sails. At this point, though, I simply don't have the energy to react—at all. Exhaustion has replaced adrenaline, and it seeps into my veins. My body is bone-tired. My head pounds so hard now that my vision is blurry. Black spots wink before my eyes, and a dull roar fills my ears, as if I'm hearing everything through an underwater filter. I can feel the cut in my forehead has re-opened as hot blood drips from beneath my bandage.

Nonetheless, Instructor Sanchez unlocks her office door, and we gather inside. After releasing Ryan's hand, I slump gratefully into a chair, and the nurse sits down next to me and grabs my arm. Her fingers rest gently on my wrist as she feels for my pulse.

"Painkillers?" I finally whisper to her, giving in to the ache in my head. "Do you have any?"

"Instructor Sanchez, Ms. Camper needs to rest," the nurse says, her hand moving to my forehead now, ignoring my question. I don't feel any strength left to my voice, and I'm not even sure she heard me.

"This will only take a moment," Instructor Sanchez answers, booting up her computer.

The nurse digs through one of her enormous pockets and pulls out a bottle, pills rattling inside. "Here," she says gently, pouring two pills out into my hand, "take these." I quickly take them from her hands and swallow them dry.

From the computer, Instructor Sanchez says, "Like I said, it's a small chance but . . ." Instructor Sanchez looks over at Ryan and me and grimaces. "As you know, as part of the Captures uniform, there is a tracker in the school crest. It's mostly to ensure student safety on missions, but it is also a way for us to monitor students if needed. We've never used it this way before, but the capability remains. It's more than likely that Kate disposed of the tracker before fleeing, so this might not work but . . ." She trails off once again and begins typing furiously into her keyboard.

"You hear that, Scarlet?" Ryan says, excitement lining his voice once again. "We might have her! She's right in our fingers!" I can't bring myself to correct him. I agree with Instructor Sanchez that Kate would have been far too clever for that. She won't let herself be found out and tracked down so easily, and to assume she was so careless is a gross underestimation of her. *Why are we all clinging to this stupid hope that we will still catch her tonight?*

"I can just go into Kate's record, and the location of her tracker should be pinged over to us," Instructor Sanchez explains, typing away and staring at her computer screen.

"Keeping our fingers crossed, eh?" Ryan said, holding up his own crossed fingers. I stare at him glumly, and his smiling face swims in and out of focus. What I wouldn't give to have that boy's optimism.

"Almost there," Instructor Sanchez reports from her desk. "And, oh. Oh!" Her eyes grow wide. "We have a signal!"

Ryan lets out an excited whoop, and I nearly fall out of my chair in shock. *What?* It has to be an error. Kate would never be so stupid. How could this be so easy?

"Zooming in on the location—drats! It's gone. We lost it." Instructor Sanchez pushes back from her desk angrily. "We had her, and then we lost her. Shoot!" Then, she swears under her breath. "She must have smashed her tracker."

I fall limply back against the nurse once again. *Knew it was too easy.*

"Are you able to go back on the map to the area where the signal was before it was lost?" Ryan asks, hope lacing his voice.

"Yes, but it won't be very accurate," Instructor Sanchez says. "Better than nothing, though. We can also try the tracker in the emergency kit if she brought that along with her. Maybe that one is still working."

But I know that Kate would have destroyed that one already. The rough map will have to be good enough.

The pills the nurse gave me seem to already be taking effect, and I push any thoughts of sleep away for the time being. Kate has slipped through our fingers before, and I won't let her do it again. This time, we will be prepared.

"We're going to need the truck."

Chapter Eight
MASKED MURDERER

SCARLET

Instructor Sanchez stares at me for a moment, her fingers steepled under her chin as she considers me.

Now that the words have left my mouth, I regret them. I probably overstepped. She's my superior and my instructor, and I need to remind myself of the hierarchy around here. I'm only a student, and I'm definitely not one who has the authority to order around an instructor or to presume that I would even come along.

"I'm sorry," I say quietly, "but we need to do something, don't we? Before we lose her," I add urgently, yet hopefully respectfully. Who knows how far Kate could have gotten after her tracker was broken? And if she had a vehicle? I don't even want to think about it. I arrange my expression into what I hope looks like polite interest and fold my hands in my lap.

Instructor Sanchez's face is inscrutable, her dark eyes betraying none of her feelings or the thoughts that I'm sure are racing through her head right now.

I wonder what the protocol for something like this is—for tracking down a student who has gone rogue. To my knowledge, nothing like this has ever happened. Maybe the headmasters have some sort of playbook for dealing with things like this. Surely, when they put together the curriculum for this school, they planned for several contingencies, including what to do if a student turned.

I open my mouth to ask if we should maybe talk to the headmasters then shut it again, giving Instructor Sanchez time to tell us her plan or to think of a plan or to dismiss us from her office . . . or do something. I chew on my lip impatiently, my polite mask slipping. At least my head has stopped throbbing thanks to the nurse's pills.

"So, what do you think, Instructor Sanchez?" Ryan asks brightly. "Let's go catch us a bad guy!"

Thank goodness Ryan asked the question I didn't want to ask. Ryan is so naïve sometimes but in a cute and charming way. If we want to get our way here, polite obedience is the way to go. Besides, doesn't he see that he and I are clearly out of our league here? Our personal connection with Kate might be more of a conflict of interest than helpful information at this point. And we might even be suspects or, at the very least people of interest, given how close we are to Kate. We need to let the professionals take it from here. We might be part of the Final Four, but we are still a long way from professional capturers.

"Ryan," I say, through gritted teeth, "we should maybe go." My mind halfheartedly buzzes around the thought of how we could be the ones to catch Kate and demand answers from her. The memory of my first capture thrills through me, but I shove it back.

"Ms. Camper, Mr. Pentaquese," Instructor Sanchez says firmly, lowering her hands to her desk. *Oh no, here it comes.*

"We are going to need guns, trackers, and knives. Change into your capturer uniforms immediately and be ready to depart in fifteen minutes. I need to make a few arrangements, and then I will meet you in the garage."

My jaw is on the floor as Instructor Sanchez turns back to her computer and begins typing rapidly. I stare at her, completely flummoxed. Did she just—

"We're coming with?" Ryan squeaks out. He sounds just as surprised and confused as I am. "On a real capture mission with you? To catch Kate?"

I wince at Ryan's questions, though they were on the tip of my own tongue. Instructor Sanchez is allowing students—allowing *us*—to come on the capture mission to catch Kate?

Instructor Sanchez clears her throat and raises a dark eyebrow at us. "I believe my instructions were clear. Go and get ready. You have nine minutes now. Don't make me regret this."

"Yes, ma'am!" Ryan salutes and makes a break for the office door before turning around, as though he had forgotten about me in his excitement about the mission. "Need some help, Scarlet?"

I grin at him. "Nope, see you in the garage!" It takes all my power to not squeak in excitement and dash out the door with him, concussion or not.

The nurse huffs and glares disapprovingly at Instructor Sanchez as she rewraps my head and gives me the entire bottle of pills, reciting their instructions and a litany of possible side effects. I barely hear her. I am going on another captures mission! I am going to help catch Kate! Then I can demand answers from her. Or maybe just cuff her, which might be more satisfying. My face lights up in a smile at the thought as I jog through the hallway to my dorm room.

Being part of the Final Four is not all sunshine and daisies. In fact, it rarely is. It's hard work and leaves me ten kinds of exhausted at the end of the day. *But this!* This is what makes it all worth it. The chance to hunt down and catch a bad guy.

Except this time, the bad guy is my best friend.

I slow my jog and sigh. Despite everything, Kate is my friend, and I just know there has to be a reason why she did all this. It's strange not knowing if I feel angry at Kate or if I want to make excuses for her. I guess, in a way, my mind needs an explanation for this—for her betrayal—because I can't believe she would do this of her own free will. I can't believe it would've been her idea to do such bloody things to another person and hurt me. My mind keeps swirling with the questions, asking if any of this is real and if our friendship was completely fake. And I hate that it matters so much to me.

I enter my room in a rush and hastily change into my uniform. I pull on my black cargo pants and black jacket. I throw my filthy shoes across the room and dig out my combat boots from the closet I share with Kate. Sitting on the floor, I lace them up over my feet. I studiously avoid looking at the smear of blood on the floor near my bed. It was a lifetime ago when I was waiting for Kate to get to class. A lifetime when we were still friends and Kate didn't whack me over the head with a pipe.

I swallow hard and grab my gloves. My dorm room door swings shut as I run through the deserted hallways. I hear a squeak behind me, like the sound of a boot on the hallway floor, but when I glance around, the hallway is deserted. Everyone must be asleep by now since it's getting late. Thank goodness because I don't have the time or the bandwidth to explain everything that has happened today.

Fresh air hits my face as I scramble outside and head over to the garage where the school's vehicles are stored. Pushing open the door, I immediately see that Ryan and Instructor Sanchez are already there, piling gear into the back of a black SUV. Both are dressed in the same clothes as me and wear grim expressions on their faces. I notice that, despite his focused and serious face, Ryan's eyes shine with excitement, and I know he feels the thrill of the capture too.

In a few minutes, the SUV is loaded with the weapons and trackers. Instructor Sanchez and Ryan take the front, and I sit in the back, fastening my seatbelt. Instructor Sanchez types a code in the dashboard electronics to start the vehicle, and the engine thrums to life with a gentle *vrooooom*.

"Open garage," Instructor Sanchez says aloud, and the metal garage doors in front of our truck begin to slide apart. We are ready to roll out. My heartbeat quickens in anticipation, and I can't help the slightly crazed smile that spreads over my face. Man, I love being a capturer.

All of a sudden, out of nowhere, the door to the truck opens and a darkly-clothed figure slides in next to me.

"Justin!" I yelp in complete shock.

He nonchalantly fastens his seatbelt. "Where are we going?" he asks, looking around the truck as if this was all planned in advance.

"Justin!" I say again. "How did—security—just get out!" I lean across him to open his door and shove him out of the truck, but he slaps my hand back, and I growl at him.

"Hey! I saw you leaving your dorm and didn't want to miss the fun. Besides, I'm also in Final Four so have just as much of a right as you do to be in this car!" Justin protests.

"I swear, I am going to—"

"Enough!" Instructor Sanchez silences us from the front seat. "If you cannot quit your bickering, I will leave you both in this garage. We are losing time to find Kate, so decide if you can act like professionals or get out now."

"Wait, what about Kate?" Justin looks confused. He and I glare at one another for a moment, and he narrows his eyes at me, as if daring me to say something and ruin my opportunity to go along on this captures mission. Fat chance of that. I resolutely cross my arms across my chest and stare at the back of Ryan's head in front of me. Justin is not going to ruin this for me. I won't let him.

"Good. We have a lot of ground to cover." Instructor Sanchez maneuvers the truck out of the garage, and the door closes silently behind us as we take off into the night.

I glance sideways at Justin. Did he know we are looking for Kate? Judging by the worry etched in every line of his face, I don't think so. I almost feel sorry for the guy. Almost.

It isn't often that we leave the mountain where the school is hidden, and I look out of the window, staring at the blurred trees whizzing past us. The last time I left the school's campus was for my first capture with Kate. Who would have ever thought the next time would be *to go capture Kate*? Anticipation courses through my veins and even though my emotions toward Kate are a tangled mess at the moment, I can't help but feel the thrill of the hunt. This is it. This is what I've been training for.

I feel ready.

The rest of the drive passes in complete silence. I'm a ball of nervous energy, and I bounce my knee and fidget with the gloves in my lap. Justin reaches over and hits me in my bouncing leg; I scowl at him. Does he have to be such a jerk all the time?

I crane my head to look up at the stars through the window of the truck. There are so many of them twinkling overhead with no light pollution out here. We seem to be heading away from the mountains and the city and into the desert. I wonder if Kate is out here and if she notices the stars too. Stargazing used to be a favorite pastime of ours, as silly as it might sound. We were two of a handful of fortunate students who had a window in their dorm room. Most of the dorms were built inside the mountain and lack any view at all. Kate and I never took our small window to the outside world for granted. We would always try to identify constellations, but neither of us was very good at it. We'd laugh at how the people who named them came up with such extravagant pictures from just a few white dots.

In a way, I guess that's what it was like to be a professional capturer—trying to pull together as many clues as possible with just a few dots of data.

Soon, the mountain landscape gives way to flatter land, and the trees thin out. The dark surroundings take on a reddish hue, and I know I'm right about the desert. We're heading to the wastelands, which are known for their red sand, sparse vegetation, and a few puddles of water here and there.

Dang. If Kate headed out to the wastelands, she must have a plan in mind since survival out here is a challenge, even for the most prepared. Or she must be very desperate. I idly wonder which it is when I spot our first clue.

"Stop!" I shout, catching everyone's attention. Instruction Sanchez skids the SUV to a halt, and I jump out of the truck onto the thick, red sand. I jog a few feet behind our vehicle back to where I saw it. Taking out my small penlight, I sweep it over the ground, and . . . *there!*

I crouch down, looking at the broken shards of our school's crest. Instructor Sanchez approaches from behind and kneels next to me.

"She was here," I murmur to Instructor Sanchez, showing her the jagged pieces of the tracker hidden in the crest. "Do you think she's still around?"

Instructor Sanchez's mouth is a thin line, and she says nothing for a moment. "Miss Camper," she says slowly, "I want you to be prepared for what we might find out here. When we find Kate, remember that she's now no longer associated with the school. The moment she made her decision to hit you and run, she forwent that association. She is no longer your classmate. She is no longer your roommate. And she is no longer your friend. Regardless of what your heart tells you." Instructor Sanchez gently puts her hand on my shoulder. "I need you to be prepared. I need you to remember that Kate is a criminal now, and you are the capturer."

My eyes don't leave the broken pieces of the tracker as Instructor Sanchez speaks. Her words drive home the point I have been trying to convince myself of for the past several hours. Her words don't convince me any more than my own do, but I nod anyway. "I understand, Instructor Sanchez," I say. "I'm prepared to do what's necessary to bring Kate in and uphold peace and justice."

I'm not sure if Instructor Sanchez believes me or not. Maybe the peace and justice bit was too dramatic. I feel her eyes drilling into the side of my head, but I keep my eyes down and focused on the broken tracker. She gives my shoulder a squeeze and turns back to the truck. "Come on," she tells me, offering her hand to help me up. "We're getting close."

We climb back into the truck, and Justin and Ryan immediately halt their conversation as soon as I open the door. My stomach twinges in irritation as I realize they were probably talking about me. Notwithstanding the fact that it bothers me any time Justin opens his stupid mouth, it bothers me that no one seems to think I can handle bringing Kate in—even though *I* am not sure I can bring her in either. Maybe if I can't talk my brain into doing this mission for myself, I can hope to at least prove them all wrong. I throw a dirty look at Justin, who blinks at me innocently, and I settle back into my seat, fastening my seatbelt once again.

"We found her tracker," Instructor Sanchez informs them.

"We must be getting close," Justin says eagerly, and I want to reach across the seat and hit him. *No duh, Justin.*

"So Instructor Sanchez and I realized, Sherlock!" I snap at him tersely before I can help myself. I flinch and glance toward Instructor Sanchez, but she doesn't say anything about Justin and me bickering.

Instructor Sanchez shifts the truck into drive again, this time keeping the headlights off so as not to give away our position. We drive slowly through the desert now, and we all are a little tenser than we were ten minutes ago.

"Keep your eyes open for anything suspicious. Any potential hiding places, clues, movement," Instructor Sanchez tells us, snapping into full-on instructor mode. She rolls our windows down so we can listen for any sounds that are out of place and to have a better view of our surroundings. The tires of the truck crunch softly over the occasional rock, but otherwise, all is silent—save for the truck's quiet engine.

I'm not exactly sure what I should be listening for. Most of our training centered on bringing criminals in from the city, not from the wastelands. I wrack my brain for any information I remember from our lessons. Should there be crickets or coyotes or something? Unfortunately, I can't remember, so I will just have to use my eyes instead.

The desert is so big. We've all studied it on maps before, but this is my first time coming out to the wastelands. The sheer vastness—and emptiness—of it is overwhelming. The red sand stretches on and on, far out of sight, and the landscape looks completely uniform. A small shrub here, a tiny copse of trees there. It would be so easy to get lost out here, and a pang of concern for Kate stabs me in the stomach, unbidden.

"Let's check out those trees," Ryan says, pointing to the small stand of trees I had just noticed. "Looks like there's a watering hole, and the trees would provide some protection. Could be an ideal shelter for someone on the run."

"Looks like a good place to hide," Justin agrees. *Shut up, Justin. No one asked you*, I think savagely, wrinkling my nose at him. I manage to keep my mouth shut this time though. Progress.

Instructor Sanchez stops the truck once again a few hundred feet away from the trees. "Alright, team," she says, and my heart swells a little at being part of her team. "We go in at different entry points. Ryan, you enter at the north. Scarlet, the south. Justin, east, and I will take west," she instructs us, and we all nod. "Let's go."

Adrenaline hits me fast and strong as we step out of the truck and break up, each approaching our own entry point. If Kate tries to run, we should have her surrounded. It's a good strategy, and I glance over to Instructor Sanchez's position with admiration.

Slowly, quietly, I creep forward toward the trees. My boots are silent on the sand, and the stars and moon above provide just enough light for me to see. I should have grabbed my night vision goggles, I think belatedly. The air is still, and not even a breath of wind disturbs the sparse trees and shrubs. A bummer because rustling leaves, even the few that are on the trees, would have been great to cover any noise our team makes as we approach. My body is amped right now, and I feel like I'm ready to take on anything that is thrown at us— including Kate. *I can do this.*

Closer and closer I sneak until I have a clear view inside the trees. My eyes take a moment to adjust to the shadows, and then I see a figure with its back to me.

Bingo.

The figure looks to be packing equipment into a travel kit. I can't see the face, but I can tell it is Kate, her movements smooth, practiced—and hurried. Did she hear us approach already? Is she about to take off now?

I slowly remove my Taser gun from my belt and crouch down, quietly moving closer to get in range. I aim it at Kate's back and close one eye, preparing to fire. My stomach is doing jumping jacks, and blood pounds in my ears. It's now or never. My finger squeezes the trigger.

But someone else beats me to it.

Zzzzzzzzzz!

Kate goes down unconscious before she even knows what hit her, and Instructor Sanchez steps out from behind a bush. Irritation burns my veins, and I scowl. I had her. I had Kate in my sights and was about to fire. She was *my* capture. Why did Instructor Sanchez step in like that?

"Target acquired," Instructor Sanchez announces, and Justin and Ryan step out of the trees.

"Wait, but we don't know who this is," Ryan exclaims as he approaches, but I know it's Kate. It has to be. She's only wearing one shoe, and I bet if I shifted her head, I would see only one earring as well. I walk over to the prone body and flip it over.

I was right. It's Kate.

"Confirmed, target acquired," I say.

Unease swirls in my belly as I take in Kate's unconscious body. It's so strange to be taking my best friend into custody as a criminal. We were always a team, completing our first capture together. And now, at our next capture, we are on opposing sides. This morning, I thought she was my friend, and now she's my enemy. Yesterday, we were eating breakfast together, and today, I was ready to use a freaking Taser gun on her, for goodness sake. I remind myself of Instructor Sanchez's words from earlier in the night. *Kate's a criminal now.* I hang on to those words tightly in my mind.

My eyes rove around the scene. It looks like Kate was going to set up camp here, but her camp is only partially assembled. Why was she packing up again already? Did she have a tip-off? Did she know we were hot on her trail?

"Let's get her back to the truck," Instructor Sanchez says, and Justin and Ryan scoop Kate up and head back to the SUV. I take the bag Kate was hastily packing and bring it along with me.

At the truck, Ryan and Justin bind Kate's hands and feet with the ropes they brought along. Instructor Sanchez, ever the teacher, examines their knots closely and pulls on them to check the tightness when they've finished. I hover awkwardly behind them, unsure of what to do or how to be useful at this point.

To be honest, I didn't expect it to be over so soon. The thought of capturing Kate has so consumed my thoughts for the few hours since she hit me over the head—gosh, has it only been a few hours?—that I haven't actually thought about what would happen once we did capture her. Of course, she will be expelled from the school, but will she wind up in jail too? I can't help but feel a little disappointed that the capture is over so quickly. I hadn't expected it to be so easy. Too easy?

Ryan and Justin situate Kate in the back of the SUV behind Justin and me, and they strap a harness across her body so she doesn't bounce around too badly back there. There is a soundproof piece of plexiglass separating Kate from the rest of us in the front of the truck, and we each glance uneasily behind us at her slumped body.

Instructor Sanchez stays outside to make a call—to the headmasters or the nurse or someone at the school, I presume—probably informing them that we captured Kate and are heading back now. They'll need to prepare the nurse and an interrogation room for her when we get back. Interrogations have never been my favorite part of being a capturer, but I am looking forward to getting some answers.

I nervously start jiggling my leg again and glance over at Justin, waiting for a snide comment from him, but his eyes are glued behind us. I notice that he shies away from Kate's unconscious body, and a petty part of me rejoices at his discomfort. Not only because I love watching him squirm but also because, now, I know it's not just me that's uncomfortable with this whole situation. I bite back the mocking words on the tip of my tongue and instead, look out the window. I should give Justin a break. After all, I'm feeling just as uneasy right now.

Although the windows are still down, Instructor Sanchez stands out of earshot on her cell phone. The wind has picked up a little bit, and waves of sand swirl and dance on the surface of the ground, making intricate designs. The wastelands really are a pretty place with their red sands and twinkling stars, and I marvel that I felt overwhelmed by them only an hour ago. I look up at the stars again and try to find the constellations Kate and I liked to point out, those tiny little dots that make such an extravagant picture. I only succeed in locating Orion's Belt, and I hope that we have an easier time connecting the dots when it comes to Kate's case.

The sound of the truck door slamming brings my head back inside as Instructor Sanchez starts the engine and punches coordinates into the truck's GPS. Now that we have our suspect, we head back to the mountains, back to school. As Instructor Sanchez swings the SUV around, I glance back at Kate and watch as her head lolls to the side. She opens her mouth in what looks like a groan.

Justin and I meet eyes in the back seat and exchange similar wide-eyed looks. I don't think either of us expected her to regain consciousness so fast.

"Um . . ." Justin begins awkwardly. "Took her long enough," he says, as Kate blinks a few times.

Kate sits up straighter in the back and rolls her head on her shoulders as if stretching her neck. I narrow my eyes at her. The movement strikes me as quite cavalier given that she's trussed up in the back of the SUV on her way to face justice for her crimes. The thought that this capture was too easy once again gnaws at me.

Kate sees me looking at her, and a smile brightens her face. She winks. *What the . . .*

"Um. I think something is wrong with Kate," I say to the rest of the team. "Does the Taser make you act all weird?"

"No," Ryan answers from the front seat, turning around to see for himself. Kate spots him and nods at him in greeting, her expression completely placid.

"Maybe she's just accepted her fate and realizes what she did was wrong. Maybe we can let her off the hook," Justin suggests, looking at Ryan and me.

"No," Instructor Sanchez says from the front. "She will face an interrogation. And if we get nothing . . ." She lets her words dangle in the air threateningly. I'm not sure how that sentence is intended to end. If we get nothing, we will imprison her? Kill her? What's going to happen? Despite myself, I shudder.

The rest of the ride back to the school is spent in terse silence. When we pull up to the garage, the doors roll apart silently, just as they had when we left.

"Stay here," Instructor Sanchez tells us. "The headmasters are supposed to meet us. I'm going to let them know we're here." She steps out of the vehicle and pulls out her phone again. The headmasters are not here yet, but I don't think I am going to like their plan. I bite my lip.

"What do you think Instructor Sanchez meant?" Ryan asks quietly. "If we get nothing, then what?" He turns around again to face Justin and me, taking care to avoid looking at Kate. "We can't let her go, but we can't just kill her, either, right? I mean, it's Kate."

"What should we do, then?" I ask Ryan as if he has a plan.

Ryan runs his hands over his face. "We should keep Kate alive no matter what, and if we don't get anything out of her the first day of interrogation, we keep her locked up until she tells us everything."

"Sounds like a plan. I'm in," I respond, still thinking this idea through. It is better than nothing, I suppose. We turn to Justin.

"I guess I'm in," Justin finally says. "As long as we keep her alive." He looks at Ryan, and then he looks at me. "One thing, though. I get to talk to her first. Alone."

CHAPTER NINE
INTERROGATIONS

JUSTIN

The room they use as Kate's jail cell is cold and dark. Everything is made of stone except for a small plexiglass window. Kate is sitting on a wooden bench attached to the back wall. When I walk in, she greets me with a smile.

"Like my new place?" she asks teasingly, nodding to her surroundings. She wears handcuffs on her wrists and shackles on her ankles and does not seem the least bit bothered by them.

The still air in the room suffocates me, and I try to take deep breaths through my nose and out my mouth. How is Kate so calm right now? This room is unnerving, which I am sure is the intention. Having such an uncomfortable interrogation room probably gets people to talk more quickly so they can get the heck out.

"Hi, Kate," I say quietly, settling into a metal chair opposite her. I notice it's bolted to the ground. I run my sweaty palms over my pants and take a deep breath.

After we arrived in the garage, Instructor Sanchez notified the school authorities. Ryan, Scarlet, and I made a plan that we would protect Kate—despite what she had done. She did not deserve death—if that indeed was the plan for her. The headmasters came along with some of the other teachers, and I had wondered why Kate, of all people, would warrant such a welcoming party. The entire time we waited for them to arrive, she had sat calmly in the back of the SUV, grinning through the window at us every once in a while. The eeriness of the interrogation room had nothing on Kate's eerie smile.

But now, she is in a cell. Where she belongs. For a while, anyway.

"What's the point?" I ask. "Why, Kate? Why did you . . ." I trail off, and a long silence lingers in the air between us. Finally, she stands up from the bench and moves toward me, keeping a respectful distance. She looks at me seriously. This is not the Kate I know.

"Everyone has a dark secret, Justin, but some aren't ready to share it," she says in a quiet voice, her eyes lowered. "But the time will come. I will know it. You will know it."

"What? What are you talking about, Kate?" I ask her. *What the heck is she talking about?* "A dark secret? What does that mean? How will I know it? Talk to me," I say urgently, leaning forward.

Kate considers me a moment and chews on her bottom lip. "If I tell you too early, this whole facility will be blown up with everyone inside it. And if I tell you too late, no cookies will be left to steal," she says with a snicker then moves back to her bench, calmly taking her seat once again with a soft sigh.

What is that all about? Is this a freaking riddle? I blink a few times and shake my head. Blowing up the school sounds straightforward enough, but what the heck does the bit about cookies mean? Is it a weird Kate expression I'm not familiar with? Is Kate trying to protect the school with her silence? A muscle in my jaw twitches as I grit my teeth in frustration.

Kate flutters her long eyelashes at me from her seat on the bench.

"I'd like to ask you a few questions," I state matter-of-factly, deciding to ignore her ominous warning—or whatever it was. I drum my fingers on the armrests of my chair.

"Okay, sure," Kate answers. She reaches her cuffed hands up and tucks a strand of hair behind her ear, the girlish gesture so at odds with our stark surroundings. For some reason, it catches me off-guard. This is a criminal, not the girl I am dating. *Are we still dating?*

I suck in a deep breath to get my bearings and think back to our interrogation training.

"Why are you so calm right now?" I ask her, my own heart pounding loudly in my chest. Hey, it's my first real interrogation after all, and the suspect happens to be the girl I should probably break up with soon.

Kate looks at me with her round, doe eyes, and I clench my jaw harder, the muscles spasming like crazy. "Because everything is going as planned," she says simply.

I think about that for a second. What does she mean by that? Is this another riddle like the cookies? *Everything is going as planned?* Does this mean—

"So your plan was to get caught?" I prompt her, resuming my finger-drumming on the armrest. "And interrogated by all your old friends, all of whom you lied to?"

"Yes," Kate answers and nods. "That's right."

Crap.

Do we really have the upper hand here or are we just playing into hers? When we made the decision to track her down and capture her? My heart sinks at the thought. Kate cocks her head at me, gauging my reaction. I must have let my poker face slip for a moment, judging by the small smirk that tugs on her lips.

"Okay," I say slowly, sliding an expressionless look over my face once again. "Why is this your plan?" I gesture widely around the room and to her cuffs.

"I can't answer that yet," Kate says plainly. She flicks a speck of dirt off her pants, the gesture useless as her pants are filthy.

"C'mon, Kate. Indulge me." I cross my arms over my chest and wait for her to respond. She simply smiles blandly at me and flicks another speck of dirt. Fine, next question then.

"It looked like you were packing to leave when we found you. Why?" I ask her.

Another bland smile.

My jaw muscle is having a full-on seizure right now.

"Did you smash your trackers or did someone else?" I go on. "That's how we found you, you know. You weren't fast enough with breaking them," I add, trying to rattle her, trying to prove that I have the upper hand in this interrogation, that we have the upper hand over her plan—that we are in control. I gaze at her intently, and she simply stares blankly back at me, not answering.

Okay. I will outlast her then. She will have to crack sooner or later. All is silent except for the steady tick of the clock on the wall, counting out the seconds of silence, then the minutes. I feel like Kate and I are in some kind of messed-up staring contest as we continue to look into one another's eyes, neither of us saying a word. My fingers resume their drumming on the armrest. In a perverted way, my memory brings me back to our first date, where we did some stupid love test. The test entailed asking each other a bunch of strange and personal questions and then gazing into one another's eyes for five minutes.

"Oh, come on," Kate had joked with me on that night, punching me gently in the arm. "It's just a fun and silly game to see if we're compatible. What's the harm? You worried we aren't?" And then she fluttered her long lashes at me and showed her perfect white teeth through a dazzling smile, and I caved and did her stupid love test.

"Okay, first," she began brightly, "Which famous figure would you invite over for dinner and why?"

"Um," I said, "I don't know. I guess Martin Luther King?"

And so on. She went through a series of questions that oscillated between the outlandishly bizarre and the uncomfortably personal.

"How do you feel?" Kate had asked breathlessly after I had stammered my way through the questions and after an excruciatingly long five minutes of eye contact at the end.

"I don't know," I had answered sheepishly. "Awkward, I guess. What am I supposed to feel?" And Kate had giggled and then thrown one of her fluffy pillows at me. We started dating after that, and I began to think that her bizarre love test might have been onto something.

Kate's stomach gives a large rumble, and the memory fades. I smirk at her. "Hungry? Would you like something to eat?" I ask innocently. This could be my leverage. This could be the way to get her to talk. Bribe her with food. Who knows when the last time was that she had a chance to eat. She must be starving with all the energy she burned today.

"I could get you a snack," I say. "Maybe some chocolate pudding? I know that's your favorite."

She shrugs. "I'm okay." Her stomach gives another loud grumble, and she winks at me. Maybe bribing her with food will not work after all. Well, we will see how she is holding up in a few hours. For now, I try another tactic.

I slap on a pained and hurt expression. "Kate, tell me what's going on," I say. "Please, tell me what you're into.

Maybe I can help you get out of it." Maybe going the pained, lovesick boyfriend route will work.

"I already told you, Justin," she says softly. "I can't answer those questions yet."

"Your trackers," I circle back, "did you smash them or not? Did someone hurt you?"

Kate suddenly drops her girlish act and bares her teeth at me in an aggressive growl. "Cut the small talk, Justin," she says in a low and dangerous voice. "I'm Final Four too, remember? I've taken the same interrogation classes as you, and I know what you're doing. Stop wasting our time."

"Kate, please," I beg, "why are you doing this? Or at least, why did you start?" I reach forward and grab her cuffed hands in my own. "Talk to me, Kate. Please." I will continue to try to play the part of scorned boyfriend here. Maybe it will get her to talk. I think I even manage to summon a tear.

"Do you not understand?" Kate snaps, her voice so sharp it could cut.

"No," I whisper. "Help me understand, Kate. What are you talking about?" I keep my hands on hers, playing my role. While I did not expect her to react so violently to the boyfriend act, it feels like I am getting close. My pulse is in my ears and my heart thuds loudly in anticipation. Maybe we will not have to starve the information out of her after all. Maybe this will be over a lot more quickly than I anticipated.

"Your sister, Justin!" Kate explodes. "Have you forgotten about her?"

I reel backward into my chair. *What the heck? My sister?* This . . . this was not what I expected.

"My sister?" I repeat blankly, forgetting my act for a moment. "I don't have a sister. You know that. You know I was adopted when I was a kid and am an only child. My parents didn't have any other kids." Remembering myself, I add pointedly, "We talked about this, remember? In our love test?" I look at her wide-eyed, fairly certain Kate has cracked. She has to be crazy. That Taser gun must have messed with her mind because I have no idea what she is talking about. I do not have a sister. I bite my cheek to hide my frustration and to stop my jaw muscle from twitching again.

"Don't you ever think about your birth parents, Justin?" Kate asks, and I'm not sure how to respond. Maybe the question is rhetorical, and I do not want to interrupt this rant that seems to be bursting to come out of Kate all of a sudden. Her face grows red and she frowns at me, narrowing her eyes. "The parents who gave birth to you," she repeats as if I am an idiot or did not hear her the first time. Whatever, I will put up with her talking down to me if it means getting answers, if it means making this interrogation a success.

I wait for her to say more, but Kate simply stares at me with her mouth pressed tightly together and her eyes narrowed skeptically at me.

"Well, who is my sister then, if you're so smart?" I demand, my impatience breaking through.

Kate smiles thinly at me. Just as she opens her mouth to answer, the door to the interrogation room swings open, and Scarlet barges in. Kate and I exchange glances, then Kate looks at Scarlet, a smug expression painted on her face.

Chapter Ten
THE REASON

KATE

I didn't always use to be like this. I didn't always use to live my life with a hidden agenda, my true motivations only fully disclosed and fractured, even in my own head. I used to trust. I used to have a family and friends who loved me. At least, I think they loved me until a point.

Could I ever have predicted that I'd wind up here? In a cell at the academy that took me in? Probably not, but it wasn't wholly unexpected. Now that I'm here, it's not so bad. I can see how each of my actions got me here, and I don't regret any of them.

I don't regret getting to know Justin and Scarlet. I don't regret kissing Justin. Hey, he is a pretty good kisser, and even if he is more into me than I am into him—well, that's just life. And too bad for Justin, but he has to grow up. Everyone experiences heartbreak at some point in their lives.

Did I ever count Scarlet as a friend? Sure. But does that mean I ever trusted her fully and told her my deep, dark secrets? No way. My secrets are mine and mine alone. In fact, my deep, dark secrets are so deep and so dark, that really, they just are a part of me now. There's no telling where they end and I begin. I am my secrets, and they are me.

My darkness has always been here, though perhaps not quite as large and hungry as it is now. I think most people have a little bit of darkness in them, which is raised and fed by the things we experience, the choices we make. And well, more bad things happened to me than most people, and in turn, I've done more bad things than most people.

Years before Scarlet and I became friends, I ran away from Captures. Alone in an endless desert, abandoned by my own family. Abandoned by Captures. I had been out there for only a night, and I knew that no one cared. No one sent out search parties. No, at most, I had been an idle thought in passing among my old peers. *I wonder what happened to that one girl. What was her name again? Oh, yeah, Kate.* Maybe if I had been out there longer, there would have been a larger response to my disappearance.

But in that endless desert, someone found me in the wild. They spoke to me, reassured me that I mattered, and eventually, took me back to the academy where I was reaccepted and taken back as if nothing had happened. As if I hadn't tried to desert them. They couldn't even summon up the energy to tell me that they cared about my life, that I mattered to them. Easier just to sweep me under the rug and pretend that it hadn't happened. Easier to go about our merry little lives and keep up appearances.

I was only in the wilderness one night, but that one night changed me. As did the person who found me. That single night in the desert revived a darker side of me, bringing to the surface the girl who I had long been forcing deep down into myself. The shadowy energies and impulses pushed against the wall that I had constructed, pushed against the smiling, happy-go-lucky girl that people at Captures thought they knew. It hammered against the persona I had so carefully put forward, and soon, cracks started to appear.

I ran away from Captures because I wanted to test something. I wanted to test just how much my absence would cost the school, the people who knew me. How big of a hole would I leave if I suddenly just up and left?

I shouldn't be surprised that the answer is that I don't matter all that much now either. This question had been answered already, but for some reason, I decided to throw a little caution to the wind and retest it. It is still true.

The shadow within me started growing long before I decided to run away, though. Years and years before that.

As a child, I was abandoned by my parents. That's when the question, *how much do I matter?* was first answered for me.

I know what you're probably thinking. *Riiiiight, Kate, I'm sure*. But it is the sad truth.

Growing up, my family was fairly close to picture-perfect. I had a mom, a dad, and an older brother, and we all lived together in your typical middle-class suburban house with a white picket fence. One of those suburbs where the grass is always bright green and everyone mows their lawns in neat little diagonal patterns. The perfect suburb where neighbors greet each other from their porches and get one another's mail and water the plants for each other when they go on vacation. A close-knit community with a carpool and a yearly garage sale.

My family was picture-perfect too. My parents were never particularly affectionate toward me or my brother, but that was okay. It was just how we were. I knew they loved me. Or, at least, I thought they did. My mom was a doctor, and my dad stayed home with my brother and me. It's not like Mom worked crazy long hours or anything. No, she was a family practitioner with a local medical group in town and worked a pretty standard nine-to-five. It's not like Dad had a drinking problem or neglected us either. Nope. Dad was pretty straitlaced and only ever even drank wine during communion when we went to Mass a few times a year. Not even a beer with the boys on football Saturdays in the fall. My brother and I even got along decently well. He was two years older than me, and while we weren't especially close, we didn't fight often. We usually just stayed out of one another's hair and kept to ourselves in our own rooms, in our own spaces. On Saturdays, our family enjoyed a routine brunch together.

Sounds completely normal and perfect, right?

That's what I thought too.

Again, I was so certain that my parents loved me, even though we weren't exactly the touchy-feely type, the type to hold hands and hug and say "I love you" every day. Some families are like that, I get it. But it just wasn't us. My parents showed me they loved me in other ways. I had my own room in our house, my own personal space, and my parents respected that. They always knocked before entering, and on the rare occasions I did get into trouble, my parents would calmly discuss my actions and their repercussions with me at our dining room table. There were never any raised voices, never any threats of kicking me out of the house. Heck, I don't even recall ever being grounded. It was always the same line: "We know you're better than your actions suggest, and we know you can and will do better." And that was that.

The truth is, I admired my parents for that line of thinking. Even though I know now that they were wrong. Because I'm not better than my actions suggest. I won't do better because I can't do better. Good grief. If my parents knew even a fraction of what I've done . . . well, let's just say that I'm not sure if even they might believe that I can do better anymore.

Anyway, this happy humdrum lifestyle went on for years and years. We stayed in that same suburban house; Mom worked her very noble job as a physician; Dad ran the house, and we ate brunch on the weekends.

Until one day, it just suddenly ended.

I was just turning thirteen, and honestly, I was not a moody teenager. I know many parents dread their kids becoming teens, but my brother was already there, and I wasn't really into the things that so many other teenagers were. I didn't have many friends at school. I was never invited to parties where there might be drinking or drugs—or invited to any parties for that matter. My grades were above average, and I was in enough clubs and extracurriculars to make myself look good on a future college application someday. Really, I was in no way a "problem child." Which makes what happened next so blinding. Maybe if I had been a bad kid, it would have made more sense. Maybe if I had been in the habit of talking back or fighting with my parents, maybe then I would have deserved what happened.

There I was, on the cusp of being a teenager, when my life completely changed.

School had just let out, and I was walking home. The warm summer air was finally dying down and transitioning into the cooler temperatures of autumn, and the leaves had only just started changing. I remember vividly walking down the sidewalk to my subdivision, under trees with mostly green leaves and the occasional burst of red or orange. None of the leaves had started falling yet. No, it was still too early in the season for that, but they would start soon. Looking back now,

I can see how I was like one of those leaves. Maybe I had not been the most vibrant or the most verdant, but this was the point at which I would start dying inside too, that I would start becoming red as blood before I fell off the tree completely, no turning back.

The sidewalks were mostly empty by the time I turned onto my block. Maybe you're thinking I felt a sense of foreboding, a sense that something was wrong, that something was off. But the truth is that I felt no such thing. It was just another normal day. I'd walk home from school, my dad would have a snack prepared for me, and I'd start on homework while we waited for my brother to get home from football practice and Mom to get home from work. I thought today would be just like that. I had no reason to believe that it wouldn't.

I trudged to my house, and all looked just as it always had. I went to the front door and turned the knob, letting myself in.

"Dad, I'm home!" I yelled, dropping my backpack by the door and taking my shoes off. Dad was always strict about no shoes in the house because we had just gotten this stupid new white carpet. Seriously, white carpet. Whatever.

But the house was empty.

And I mean, completely empty.

"Dad?" I called. I moved out of the entryway into the living room. The room was totally bare. The furniture was gone. There were no family pictures on the walls. Everything was just . . . gone. Not even a dust bunny hiding out in the corner. It was as if no one had ever lived there at all.

I used to watch shows on television where a couple would try to find the perfect house to buy. It was something my dad and I did together, kind of our thing. The television couple would always have conflicting styles and priorities and visit several different houses. My dad and I would try and guess which one they would end up picking. The houses were always empty of furniture, a blank canvas full of opportunity, just waiting for the couple to put their own mark on it.

That's what my house felt like. Except that the blank canvas of opportunity felt so wrong. Instead of possibility, there was only emptiness.

"Dad? What's going on? Where is everything?" I don't know why I kept calling for my dad. If he hadn't answered on my first call, I knew he was probably not home.

Still, I didn't feel any foreboding. Mostly, I just felt weirded out. Maybe I wasn't in the right house. Maybe I had accidentally gone into a neighbor's house or something. But when I went into my bedroom and all my things were still there, I knew it was my house.

Why was everything else gone but my room completely untouched? My bed was still made from when I had done it that morning. My silly stuffed animals still sat neatly on the shelves, and the screensaver on my computer played a slide-show of pictures.

Frowning, I went down the hall to my brother's bedroom. Maybe Mom and Dad were out getting new furniture or something to redo the main areas of our house. My brother's door was open, and before I even poked my head inside, I could see that had also been emptied of everything, just like the rest of the house.

I took out my cell phone and went to my contacts, pressing Dad's name. I held my phone up to my ear, waiting for him to pick up. On the other end of the line, the phone rang once before I heard a robotic voice: "The number you are trying to reach has been disconnected."

What the heck? I lowered my phone and stared at it as if it held the answers. I tried Mom's number. Same message. My finger hovered over my brother's number next, but I couldn't bring myself to hit CALL. He was at football practice, I told myself. He wouldn't be able to answer anyway. I'll just wait for him to come home, and maybe, he will know what is going on.

I retrieved my backpack from where I had dropped it by the front door and moved to where our dining table used to be. I stood there awkwardly for a moment and then sat on the floor, pulling out my notebooks and textbooks. Might as well start on my homework.

Despite everything, despite that my house was completely empty of furniture except for my room, that my dad might be missing, and that I couldn't get ahold of my parents, I didn't have any trouble focusing on my homework. I went through my math sets and answered reading questions, and it wasn't until my stomach growled that I paused. I glanced at the clock on the oven. It was nearing 5:00 p.m. now, and my mom and brother would be home soon. *Should be home soon.* Usually, Dad would have started making dinner by now. My stomach rumbled loudly again. Maybe Mom would bring home take-out or something, I thought. Ever health-conscious, we didn't eat takeout often—just on special occasions like road trips, and sometimes, we would order pizza for birthdays or celebrations. I put my schoolwork back in my bag and padded back over to the front door.

Our door had a pane of glass next to it, which gave me a clear view of the sidewalk in front of the house. I set my backpack down and sat on the floor in front of the door, watching and waiting for my brother and Mom to get home. At this point, curiosity gnawed at my brain. This whole missing furniture thing and my parents' phones being accidentally disconnected—because I was positive that it was all an accident—was one big mystery, and I was looking forward to Mom explaining it to me. I pictured myself slapping my hand to my forehead and it all making sense.

So I sat there and waited. And waited. And waited. I didn't have a clear view of a clock, and I had left my phone on the dining room floor, so I don't know how long I sat there. My butt started to go numb from the hardness of the floor, and my legs had long since fallen asleep. Still, I kept my vigil. I watched through the window and waited. The light began to fade outside as the sun went down. With autumn approaching, the days were growing shorter and shorter.

No Mom. No Dad. And my brother never came home either.

Night had truly fallen, and still, I waited there on the floor. I don't remember if my mind was buzzing about where they were, about where our furniture had gone, or about anything that was happening. I don't remember much about those hours I sat there, staring out the window by the front door. My mind wasn't jumping to conclusions; I didn't think anything had really happened. I was only confused and curious.

Eventually, I fell asleep on the floor. I don't know how long I had been dozing, but I woke up when an owl hooted loudly outside. I blinked a few times, for a moment disoriented, wondering why I was slumped on the floor in the entryway, before my memory of the evening returned. It didn't come back and hit me in a rush. It was more of a simple realization: "Oh yeah, this is still happening." What did hit me was my hunger. I hadn't eaten since lunchtime at school, and I was also incredibly thirsty.

It was only then I finally got up off the floor and abandoned my watch. In the kitchen, I opened up the refrigerator, looking for a snack or maybe some leftovers that I could heat up. The fridge was, of course, empty. What's more is that the fridge light did not turn on when I opened it. Strange, I thought. My stomach rumbled loudly, and I thought maybe I could run out to McDonald's or something and grab a hamburger if it wasn't too late. I wondered what time it was, and I glanced over at the digital clock on the oven. It was blank.

Super weird, I thought. I knew it had been working earlier that day. I tried the kitchen light switch, but the lights didn't turn on. I flicked the switch a few times just to make sure. Nope. Our electricity was off.

I grabbed my phone to check the time. Luckily, it still had half the battery left. It was just after midnight. I opened up the internet browser on my phone to see if the McDonald's near my house might still be open so I could have a very late dinner. I waited for my browser to load.

"You've got to be kidding me," I said, as I received a *this page cannot be displayed* message. In addition to no electricity, I had no phone service either, apparently.

Cursing, I decided to go to bed hungry. I filled a glass of water (thank heavens our water still worked) and shuffled to my bedroom. Without even bothering to get undressed, I pulled the covers over me, buried my face in my pillows, and cried.

I don't know what it was that finally broke me. I cried because I was hungry. I cried because there were no lights on in my house. I cried because I missed my brother and my parents. I cried because I was alone. I cried because I knew, deep down, they weren't coming back for me.

Experiencing the trauma of being abandoned as a child by my parents, my faith in others was shattered.

I didn't go to school the next day. Or ever return to school. No one ever called our landline or came to check on me. It was like my family and I didn't exist anymore.

I never saw my parents again.

And I vowed to never trust another soul ever again either. If my own family could just up and abandon me as if I had never even been a part of their lives, I couldn't see how I would be able to trust someone else. If my own blood left me, surely I could not count on anyone who didn't share my DNA.

I don't remember how long I stayed in my abandoned house with no electricity or no food before I went to Captures. It could have been only a few days, or it could have been months. That part of my life is just a black spot that I don't want to try to remember.

What I do know is that darkness grew inside me. It grew and grew, and I fed that darkness with hatred toward my family. And with hatred toward myself—convinced that, somehow, I must not have been good enough for my family to take me with them.

Some people's minds might play tricks on them. They might doubt what they ever had was real or not. Not me, though. I knew it was real. So I fed the darkness inside me with more anger, more distrust, and more hate. But, eventually, the darkness desired more.

It wanted blood.

Chapter Eleven

5:08

Scarlet

I had hovered outside the cell, taking in the scene through the one-way glass. I had heard everything. Every single word. I have never been great at interrogations, and begrudgingly, I accept that Justin may excel at this far more than I do. Justin had called first dibs on interrogating her "alone," and Ryan and I had agreed. But there was no way I was going to let Justin go completely on his own. I am more involved in this than he is. The throbbing bump on my head is proof of that. And so, I hid in the observation room and turned on the mic.

As Justin interrogated Kate, every word was audible to me. I wish it wasn't. I wish I hadn't heard. Maybe I could ask someone to hit me over the head again and hope for some amnesia, something to wipe away the memory. My head pulsed painfully at the thought.

Instead of pulling Justin out of the interrogation room, I decide to step in. Just at the right and wrong time. I wonder what is going through Kate's head as I walk in. Does she know I was listening on the other side of the window? I can't imagine how she might know. Maybe she just took a lucky guess that I was watching and listening.

While I care very little about Justin's home life, whether he has siblings or not (honestly, let's be real, I frankly couldn't care less about anything Justin-related), I can't shake the feeling Kate gives me as I walk into that room. I didn't know Justin had been adopted, so the fact that he might have a long-lost sister means little to me—until I see this look from Kate. The one with the raised eyebrow and crooked grin. This look that seems to insinuate that *I* am connected to the whole thing somehow. That *I* am Justin's sister.

Which is impossible.

Right?

———

Questions buzz in my brain though it has been hours since the interrogation. I drum my fingers on the desk in a pattern that has no rhythm, beats that have no connection, just like the thoughts racing through my head. I'm sitting in the computer lab down the hall from the interrogation cells.

This is where we process interrogation notes. I suppose it looks a bit like the inside of a police station, at least from what I've seen on television. There are a few desks with state-of-the-art computers boasting high-tech surveillance add-ons. As part of Captures, we use this lab to process surveillance footage, check satellite images, and replay interrogation audio.

I glance at the clock glowing on the wall. It's nearly 5:00 a.m., and I know I need to get some sleep. But that will have to wait for now. There are way too many questions lingering in my head, and Kate's smug expression as I entered the interrogation room swims in front of my vision.

Tap, tap, tap go my fingers on the desk, and I bite my lip as I consider what I overheard. I chew on my lip even harder as my finger lingers over the play button on the interrogation audio file. Apparently, I'm a glutton for punishment and torturing my poor self because before I can stop myself, I hit the play button again. I close my eyes as I imagine the scene and listen.

"Your sister, Justin! Have you forgotten about her?"

"My sister? I don't have a sister. You know that. You know I was adopted when I was a kid and am an only child. My parents didn't have any other kids. We talked about this, remember? In our love test?"

"Don't you ever think about your birth parents, Jus—"

I pause the audio and rub my temples. A headache is forming behind my eyes, and it's not from my concussion. Was that seriously less than a day ago? So much has happened in the past twenty-four hours.

I roll my head on my shoulders, and my neck cracks. I lick my lips, which are raw from all my chewing. I should get some water. I'm sure the nurse would yell at me about the importance of rest and hydration to my recovery and how if I wasn't obeying the order to rest, I could at least try to stay hydrated.

I crack my neck again and get to my feet, heading to the door of the lab. I peek out into the hallway to see if anyone is here, though I doubt it. It's too early. Captures is asleep and anyone out on missions for the night will not start trickling back in for another hour or so.

I head over to a drinking fountain down the hall and, for a brief moment, I contemplate heading back to my dorm room and getting some shuteye. My head feels so heavy from exhaustion, my injury, and the weight of so many questions pulling me down. I really need answers, and I doubt that sleep will come to me.

At the drinking fountain, I bend down and take a few sips of water. How did Kate find out? How did she know? What else does she know? Could Justin really be my brother? For as long as I can remember, I've always thought I've had no family, not even parents. And now I have a brother—allegedly. Not even some random brother, but it's someone that I know. Someone who has been part of my life—and not in a good way. It's so wild, and my thoughts spin so fast, I feel dizzy.

I need to talk to Kate. Alone. Given the time, that shouldn't be a problem since Instructor Sanchez won't start her interrogation until later in the morning, and Ryan and Justin have long since gone to bed. Though how they can sleep after this night is beyond me.

I wipe my mouth and stride to Kate's cell. Maybe she's bluffing. It's stupid of me to be so shaken up about it, to be so preoccupied about words that probably mean nothing at all. Words without merit and intended only to rattle me, to keep me on my toes and off-kilter.

I slow my pace for a moment, but I don't stop. Those answers? I need them now. I can't just write off Kate's words as lies or the ravings of a crazy girl. I recall my training and square my shoulders. I need to take this seriously and take Kate's words at face value until I find out the deeper meaning.

This is my mission, and I'm not sure that it's something the Captures administration would approve of. I need to do this before anyone else comes to interrogate Kate. Or finds me here since surely having students in this building interrogating other students at five in the morning is another thing the school administration is unlikely to approve.

Outside Kate's door, I hear her softly humming. Oddly, for a split second, the sound comforts me, and I'm transported back into our dorm room only a few weeks ago as we sang into hairbrushes and danced around together in our pajamas, acting silly like only best friends can. Kate is actually a pretty good singer, but she would sing wildly off-key sometimes to make me laugh, and it cracked me up every time. One time, I was doubled-over laughing so hard that I snorted and sounded just like a pig, and that got Kate going too. Both of us collapsed onto the floor of our dorm room in hysterical giggles. It took us nearly ten minutes to catch our breath.

A fond smile starts to curve my lips before I remind myself that version of Kate isn't here anymore. This humming is not the humming of my former friend and classmate. This is a cold-blooded killer who tried to kill *me* too.

Focus, Scarlet, focus.

I pause outside the door. *Last chance to turn back, Scarlet. Just turn around and pretend that this never happened. Go back to your dorm room, forget about Kate's words, forget about Justin, and maybe you'll wake up and find this has just been a horrible nightmare.*

I scan my finger and the door to Kate's cell unlocks. I take a deep breath and decisively pull the door open and walk in. No turning back now.

"I expected you a bit earlier," Kate says by way of greeting. I say nothing, merely staring at her. I sit down in the chair opposite her and cross my arms around me. After a moment, she resumes her humming. Although the cell is dark, Kate's eyes are shiny and bright despite the black circles under her eyes. She must be exhausted too. If she's tired and not thinking straight, maybe I can use that to my advantage.

"What?" I finally say, keeping my arms crossed. My muscles are already starting to feel stiff from holding this position, trying to convey casual disinterest.

Kate pauses her humming after a few more bars. With a jolt, I realize it's the song from a few weeks ago, the one we sang and danced and laughed to. I swallow.

"I know what you want to know," she answers. Her voice has a singsong quality to it. "But I can't tell you that."

"Why not?" I ask evenly. I remind myself not to show how much I deeply desire this information. My arms remain crossed and my face passive.

"Well, you might think of it as Justin's business," Kate says slowly, "but as a matter of fact, Justin's business, in this case, includes you too. So maybe I'll relent."

"I have no idea what you're talking about," I lie. "So I am going to ignore that. I have some questions of my own for you."

Kate rolls her eyes at me. "I know, I know," she says, picking at a loose string on her sleeve. "You want to know about everything, I'm sure. And I'm sure you're wondering, *why, Kate, why?* But the only thing I will tell you is the answer to 'Justin's business.'"

"I don't care about Justin's business. That has nothing to do with why I'm here," I say, inflecting a bite into my voice. Let her believe I'm getting frustrated with all her talk of Justin. Let her think that it's something else that I'm after. "My first question for you is—"

"It may have more to do with you than you think," Kate interrupts, holding her calm tone, though I hear an edge creep into it. *Bingo.* I'm close now. "Justin's your brother."

And even though I had already overheard her insinuate this to Justin, even though I already suspected that's what she meant with her strange look, even though I had already been playing through this scenario in my head for hours, I am still caught off-guard.

Justin's your brother. To hear the words said aloud is like a sledgehammer to my gut, and all of a sudden, I feel like I am about to throw up.

I abruptly stand up, and the room around me spins. Without another word, I leave Kate's cell, shutting her alone in the darkness.

Justin's your brother. Justin's your brother. JUSTIN'S YOUR BROTHER.

I make it to a trash can near the drinking fountain before I vomit. The bile leaves a sick taste in my mouth, but that's nothing compared to the sick feeling Kate's words have left swirling through my head and heart.

Kate is lying. She has to be. There's no way. Finding out that my archnemesis from school who is—was, I keep doing that—dating my ex-best-friend-turned-murderer is my long-lost brother is way too much of a soap opera story for real life. This has to be a lie. Part of Kate's strategy to keep us—to keep me—distracted and off-balance so she can carry out whatever her plans may be.

I grip the edge of the trash can. I got the information I needed, didn't I? Why do I still feel so uneasy? Was it selfish of me to interrogate Kate, a known killer, on personal matters?

Shouldn't I have been trying to find out more information about her other crimes? Maybe figure out a motive or who she is working with? What if it's all connected, my alleged siblinghood with Justin? But *how*?

And what if it's true? My stomach churns and my mouth starts to water. I hold myself over the trashcan and hurl once more.

Is it really be so bad? To be Justin's sister?

Um, yes, it is because Justin is a total douche. I cannot stand the thought of us sharing blood. Oh my gosh. If Kate's words are true, then Justin is the only person in the world that I know to be connected to me by blood. I shake my head as I brace myself over the trash for another bout of vomiting.

I need to talk to Justin. Maybe he has more information or clues that can help me debunk this ridiculous notion that we're related. He was Kate's boyfriend, after all—maybe he knows her in a way that I don't, understands her from a different angle. As much as I detest working with him, I am prepared to do it to get to the bottom of this.

Once I'm fairly positive that I'm not going to hurl again, I adjust my ponytail and take a few gulps of water, swishing it around my mouth. I pop one of the pain pills that the nurse gave me earlier and wash it down with more water before heading over to the dorms.

As I walk toward the student living section of our school, I glance out the window. It's still dark outside, but to the east, the sky has turned a bit gray as the sun prepares to rise. *What a long freaking day.*

When I arrive at the dorms, I march down the boys' corridor, reading the names on the doors as I go. At Justin's name, I stop and crack my knuckles. It's now or never.

I pound on his door with my fist. "Justin!" I shout through the door. "Justin, open up!" Not willing to wait, I try the doorknob, and surprisingly, it's unlocked. Who in the world is part of a law enforcement agency like Captures and sleeps with their door unlocked?

I slam open Justin's door, and it bangs off the wall.

"Justin!" I yell, not caring that I'm waking up his roommates.

"Dude, what the heck?" one of his roommates grumbles at me. "It's frickin' five in the morning. What's your problem?"

From one of the beds, a pillow is thrown and hits me in the shoulder. Rude. "Justin! I need to talk to you. Now!"

"Can't it wait?" Justin mumbles from the far corner of the room.

"Now!" I roar.

"Justin, get her out of here," the pillow-thrower mutters.

These boys are a bunch of babies, that's for sure. Our morning wake-up call is in an hour anyway. I'm sure they don't whine at any of the instructors for waking them before they can finish getting their precious beauty sleep. An image of Instructor Sanchez dealing with their morning grumbles alights in my mind, and I can't help but grin. She would not take their nonsense.

"Justin, hurry up!" I flick the light switch on and off, and the room flashes. More grumbles emerge from the boys. In my foul mood, I have to admit that ticking them off is giving me a small sense of satisfaction.

Finally, Justin stumbles out of his bed. "I'm coming, I'm coming. Jeez," he says, glaring at me. He pulls a sweatshirt on over his pajamas and sneakers. He's barely done lacing his shoes up before I grab his hand and pull him out of the room, slamming the door once again on his confused roommate.

"What the heck is your problem?" Justin asks, trying to rub the sleep out of his eyes with one hand. "You should go to bed. You look terrible."

A muscle in my cheek twitches, but I say nothing.

"Like, you look like you haven't slept in days," he continues. "Might I recommend a solid night's sleep? I hear it's a lovely thing that helps you deal with trauma. I wouldn't know exactly since my solid night's sleep was interrupted by some lunatic girl banging on my door at five in the morning."

I feel Justin glaring at me, and I'm sure that he can feel the loathing that rolls off me toward him. Still, I don't respond to him. This is much more important than my and Justin's bickering. Even if he is being colossally rude.

I drag Justin all the way back to the interrogation center, back to Kate's cell, and he complains the entire way. I think, *there's no way someone this whiny can be related to me.*

Once we get to Kate's cell, I notice she has stopped humming. Good, at least that will help me keep my head on straight and not lose myself in nostalgia and rose-colored happy memories. I shudder. The humming unnerved me more than I had thought.

I scan my thumbprint over the keypad and hear a soft click as the door unlocks. I throw open the door. Justin needs to hear this. Maybe he has more insight than I do. Maybe he can fill in some of the blanks in my head. Maybe he has the facts and the proof to poke holes in this stupid lie that we're siblings or even distantly related. Clearly, he hasn't truly thought through the implications of Kate's words, given that he was sleeping like a baby only a few moments ago.

"Kate," I yell, as we barge into the cell. "Tell Justin what you just told—" I stop midsentence.

"Wait . . . where is she?" Justin says. He turns to me and eyes me suspiciously, all sleep gone from his face now. "You got me out of bed for this? An empty cell? Are you messing with me?"

"Shut up," I snap. "You know she was here. You were just here earlier tonight." I look around the empty room.

Completely empty. My brain registers the clock on the wall, taunting me with dim red numbers: 5:08 a.m.

"She's gone," I say. "Kate's gone."

CHAPTER TWELVE
LOST BUT NOT FOUND

RYAN

Since we captured Kate, Scarlet has been strange. Maybe it is the concussion. Or maybe it is the fact that the concussion was caused by her at-the-time-BFF. Even though Kate has been here only one night as a "bad guy," Scarlet has had some serious attitude changes. I know I haven't been at this school for very long, but I also know that I have a good understanding of most of the people here. I won't be coy enough to leave out the fact I've been paying extra-close attention to Scarlet. Something has been bugging Scarlet, and I'm curious to get to the bottom of it.

These are the thoughts that have been racing through my mind over and over again like cars zooming in a never-ending circuit around a racetrack. After we managed to capture Kate, our little team breaks up to regroup. I head back to my dorm room, one hundred and fifty percent exhausted. My head hits the pillow, but I can't shut the thoughts off for ages. What's on Scarlet's mind? What possessed Kate to do what she did? How can I help Scarlet? Eventually, my weary body overtakes the thoughts, and I drift into an uneasy and fitful sleep.

That night, I dream of Scarlet. She sits on the bed in her dorm, and I sit across from her, facing her, holding her hands, and looking into her eyes. We laugh together like we're friends or something more. There's an intimacy between us, like I could tell this girl anything and know she'd be on my side. I tell a joke in the dream, and Scarlet throws back her head and lets out a squeal of mirth as though it's the funniest thing she's ever heard. The warmth in my chest blossoms even larger. Scarlet looks at me from across the bed again, only blood starts to drip from her forehead and down her face. Her expression is still frozen in a huge smile, but more and more blood falls from her head, washing down her face. So much blood. Scarlet suddenly falls off the bed.

I watch myself shout in alarm and scramble up. Behind Scarlet lurks a huge figure with a giant pipe in hand. From the end of the pipe, Scarlet's blood drips in a bright red staccato onto the floor. I want to scream at the figure, to tackle this attacker, but I can't move. And suddenly, it's Kate's face on the attacker's, and instead of Scarlet on the floor, it's a corpse from the sewers with all of the blood drained out.

The next thing I hear is an alarm blaring, penetrating my nightmares about dead bodies and sewers and backstabbing friends.

It takes me a minute before I realize the alarm is not part of my dream and not my alarm clock going off to wake up for class and training. No, this is the schoolwide alarm signaling there's an emergency, that something bad has happened.

I blink the sleep out my eyes and dizzily sit up, half expecting an attacker holding a pipe to be there in my dorm room with me.

"*Escape. This is not a drill. Escape. Escape,*" comes a calm, monotonal voice from the school's speakers.

What? Escape? I shake my head to try to clear away my dizziness and roll out of bed. I shuck off my pajamas and throw on clothes, lacing up my boots on the way out the door.

The light in the hallway blinds me for a moment compared to the darkness of my dorm room.

What time is it? What's going on?

Curious faces poke out of the other dorm rooms in my hallway, and students make their way to the cafeteria, per our protocol, most still in their pajamas.

Who knew those emergency drills would one day come in handy? I rub my eyes and join the crowd. I make it only a few steps before I suddenly stop, my sleepy thoughts finally awakening and catching up with me.

"Dude, don't stop in the middle of the hallway. Keep moving!" A rough hand shoves me, and I stumble forward a step.

"Escape. Escape. This is not a drill."

I narrow my eyes. I have a sinking feeling that Kate might have something to do with these unprecedented circumstances, with this "not-a-drill-escape" message.

I turn away from the crowd and go in the opposite direction. Thankfully, most people ignore me, too tired or too confused to really care where I'm headed.

I jog to the place where Kate is being held. The alarm echoes around me, and I quicken my pace. *"Escape. Escape. Escape."* My heart beats harder and more quickly as my thoughts begin their familiar trek around the racetrack in my mind.

I fling the door open to the holding area and nearly hit Instructor Sanchez.

"Instructor Sanchez," I gasp. "I am so sorry. I . . ." My mortified apology trails off as I realize she barely notices me. Her face is red with anger, and that anger is directed toward Scarlet and Justin at the moment.

"I'm sorry!" Scarlet sputters. "I just wanted our conversation to stay inside the cell." She hangs her head, and her long ponytail falls to the side.

"That move was stupid, and you knew it was," Instructor Sanchez rages. A vein throbs in her forehead, and I'm grateful that I'm not the subject of her ire.

"We're so, *so* sorry," Justin agrees, a pink flush around his neck creeping up to his ears.

Instructor Sanchez glares at the pair of them, and before I can think, I open my mouth and ask, "What—what happened?"

Three pairs of upset eyes turn toward me in slow motion, and Scarlet arches an eyebrow at me.

"*Escape. This is not a drill. Escape. Escape,*" the alarm continues.

"Did . . . uh, did Kate get out or something?" I add hastily.

There's a moment of silence that lasts just long enough for the stupidity of my question to sink in.

Scarlet snorts loudly. "Yes, idiot. Why else would we be here?" she snaps. Even Justin looks at me incredulously.

"Um, yeah—I don't know," I stammer.

Instructor Sanchez thankfully intervenes. "Why aren't you in the cafeteria with the other students?" she asks me pointedly. "Of course," she answers herself before I can get a word out. "You're just as invested in this as your classmates now, aren't you?"

I simply nod and keep my mouth firmly closed.

Instructor Sanchez sighs heavily and throws her hands in the air. "Come on then, you three. Let's go track her. But remember," she says with a long look at Scarlet, "you are walking on eggshells right now."

Instructor Sanchez leads us down the hallway to the navigation board, and we follow her into a small, dark room. The door swings shut heavily behind us, and I jump a little. I can't help it. I feel so on edge now that the events of last night, once again, feel all too close. It makes me miss my warm bed, where it was still possible to hope that this had all just been a dream.

The room is filled with computers, and screens line the entirety of one wall. We've learned how to track in our classes, and I pull up a chair to the nearest computer, my training kicking in despite my shock and exhaustion.

"So, Kate was last in holding," I think aloud as I log into the computer with my school credentials and pull up our tracking software. "And you saw her how long ago?" I prompt Justin and Scarlet.

Scarlet and Justin exchange a look, and I frown. What's going on with those two? I never would have thought that they would be on the same side of anything.

"An hour?" I press them. "More? Less?"

"About an hour, yeah," Justin says slowly.

"So she can't have gone far on foot," I say, clicking and dragging up a map. "Let's put in coordinates here around the school to limit the search."

"Ryan," Scarlet says through gritted teeth. "I appreciate you and all, but do you have to narrate every frickin' thing you are doing right now?"

My face falls. Seriously, what is with her? Some of my hurt must show on my face because a moment later, she apologizes. "I'm sorry. You're trying to help—and you are—but just . . . my head is killing me. Can we just please try to hurry?"

I don't respond and turn back to the computer screen, swallowing down my hurt feelings. *It's just the circumstances, Ryan,* I tell myself. Scarlet is just on edge because of the circumstances. It's getting to her. It's getting to all of us.

"Do a pull of security cameras around the school for any face matches from the last hour or so. We know she disabled the camera outside the holding cell, but maybe there are some she overlooked," Instructor Sanchez says, leaning over me to look more closely at the screen.

I doubt that Kate would have let herself be caught on any of the school's security cameras, but I'm not about to question my teacher at the moment. I do as I'm told and click into Kate's student file. I pull up her school photo and run it through the image recognition software. The computer scans through the last hour of footage for any matches to Kate, but I'm not holding my breath.

To my surprise, there's a match.

To my even greater surprise, Kate's still in the school.

Instructor Sanchez swears. "What is she up to?" she says, to herself or to me, I'm not quite sure.

"That's the first-year wing," Justin says, crowding over the computer now as well. I glance over at him. He's chewing on his lip, a faraway look in his eyes. I have been so busy wondering about the effect that Kate's betrayal would have on Scarlet that I didn't think about what it might be doing to my friend Justin. He must be having thoughts and emotions similar to Scarlet's. Was his relationship with Kate real? Did anyone know the real Kate anyway? My stomach twinges as I remember the strange look that passed between Scarlet and Justin earlier. My poor friends.

Kate did this to them. Kate betrayed them, took their love and affections, and then stabbed them both in the back, twisting the knife. And neither of them saw it coming. What kind of person can do that? My mind drifts to the body in the sewers, though I never actually saw it, and the twinge in my stomach turns into a full roil. Evil. Just evil.

I decide then that if I ever get to Kate, she will pay. She will pay for what she's done to that poor soul in the sewers, and she will pay for the agony she has put my friends through.

"What are we waiting for?" Scarlet says impatiently. "Let's go get her! She's right there." Scarlet claps me on the shoulder, but instead of the warm and secure feeling I want from her touch, I just feel hollow inside.

"Zoom in on that camera just north of there," Instructor Sanchez tells me, pointing at the screen. "That one, right there."

A few keystrokes and clicks, and the camera adjusts and zooms in. It's pointing into a classroom, and just in frame is Kate. She sits on a desk in the otherwise empty room, her arms wrapped around herself. I squint at the picture. She appears to be alone and just *sitting there*. The quality of the picture is too grainy to make out much at such a zoomed-in view, but Kate looks dejected. Her eyes are drawn downward, and she seems deflated, as though she has no fight left in her.

Why would she go to all the trouble of breaking out of the holding cell only to hang out in a classroom? Truly bizarre. What is her scheme? It has to be part of some plan.

"She appears to be alone," Instructor Sanchez mutters. "It seems as though it would be safe to approach." She stands upright and looks at the three of us. "Do I have a volunteer?"

"Me!" Scarlet and Justin say together before the question has barely left Instructor Sanchez's mouth. They glare at one another.

"I think I deserve this more than you do, Scarlet," Justin says flatly. "I've earned this."

"Oh, ho! You think so, do you?" Scarlet shoots back at him fiercely.

"Mr. Pentaquese, thank you for volunteering," Instructor Sanchez says wearily, kneading her forehead.

Scarlet's and Justin's mouths drop open, and as one, they turn to me. Neither of them dares to protest.

"Be sure to take your Taser with you and be ready to call for backup if you need it. We will be down the hall awaiting your signal should you be in any distress or encounter any danger," Instructor Sanchez went on. I notice that she doesn't include Kate in her "any danger" remark.

I stand up and nod. "Okay," I say simply. "I'm ready."

"I'll grab you a Taser. Hang tight for a moment," Instructor Sanchez says and walks over to a locked closet and rifles through it.

My eyes meet Scarlet's, and she offers me a steady smile. "You're ready," she repeats to me. She takes a tentative step toward me and blows out a breath. "Listen, I'm sorry for losing my temper. I feel bad about that. That was out of line."

"Hey, it's okay," I say softly. "We all have rough days, and we all know your day has been rougher than most."

"It's not okay," Scarlet says forcefully, and I blink in surprise. "It's not okay. There's something I have to tell you. I . . . um—well . . ." Scarlet blows out another puff of air and starts fiddling with the end of her ponytail.

I reach out and grab her wrist to stop her fidgeting. "Scarlet," I say quickly before I chicken out. The next words out of my mouth might be stupid, but I don't care. They come out in a rush. "Scarlet, I care for you. I like you. Like, *like* you."

Scarlet freezes. *Oh no,* I think to myself. That was stupid. I hope that I didn't just ruin things between the two of us. I swallow.

"You do?" Scarlet says softly, staring at my hand lingering on her wrist for a moment before meeting my eyes again.

"I do," I say quietly. "When this is all over, we should go into town and see a movie or something."

She laughs, and the sound is the most amazing thing to my ears. "I would like that." She flings her arms around my neck and embraces me in a tight hug. "I would like that a lot," she says into my ear, her breath warm on my neck. I hug her back, and holding her in my arms is a balm for my exhaustion and the doubts peppering my mind. I can do this. And when it's all over, this girl who is like none other I have ever met wants to go on a date with me. My chest swells with joy, and a ridiculous smile plasters itself over my face. The racing thoughts in my head, which haven't been quiet since this Kate situation started, stop on their track and marvel.

I squeeze Scarlet tighter in my arms. This girl has been through so much in the last twenty-four hours, and the fact that she is still standing here, ready to go confront the person who hurt her so badly, emboldens me. This girl is incredible, and I would do anything for her.

Justin clears his throat loudly, and my rosy thoughts start to gray around the edges. "Whenever you're ready," Justin says snidely.

"Why bro? Why you gotta be like that?" Scarlet's voice is muffled against my shoulder, but she releases me and turns to Justin. "Can't we just get a second?"

"Excuse me, but we have a bad guy to catch," Justin says pointedly.

Right on cue, Instructor Sanchez turns around from the closet and comes back over, pressing a Taser into my hand.

"I've just let the headmasters know the full situation," Instructor Sanchez says, her fingers brushing over the cell phone hooked to her belt, "and they will hold the rest of the students in the cafeteria for now and not intervene. This is your shot." She looks from me to Scarlet to Justin, meeting each of our eyes in turn, making sure we understand the gravity of her words. "Make it count."

It still doesn't feel entirely fair that it should be me confronting Kate right now. Justin had a more personal connection to her. Scarlet had a more personal connection to her.

But maybe that's why it's me. Maybe Kate will see me as a more objective person precisely because she and I don't really have that same level of emotional connection. It sure seems like a heck of a lot to gamble on if that is the logic behind Instructor Sanchez's decision to send me in.

Instructor Sanchez hands me an armored vest, and I slip it over my head. She starts buckling the straps around my chest and waist, making sure it fits snugly and covers my vital organs.

Ah, maybe Instructor Sanchez isn't so confident that Kate is not a danger after all.

"You know the distress signal?" Instructor Sanchez asks me. I nod, and she continues. "You won't be alone in there. We have your back. Your primary objective is to bring Kate in alive and unharmed. Take your time."

"I will, Instructor Sanchez," I say. She claps me on the back and motions toward the door.

The four of us move out and head toward the first years' wing of the school. Instructor Sanchez leads the way, holding a small tablet on which she is monitoring Kate's location as we walk. The halls of the school are the same as they always are, and it almost feels as though I'm just walking to class on the morning of a regular school day. The weight of my armored vest could almost be my backpack.

Next to me, Scarlet's hand brushes mine. I glance at her, and her mouth quirks up in a grin before she grabs my hand in hers.

Hand-in-hand, Scarlet and I walk down the hall together, and despite everything, my heart blooms as if Scarlet has transferred some of her own resilience and courage to me with the gesture. Am I nervous about what's to come? Of course. But with Scarlet by my side, the rosiness has returned to my thoughts.

We turn down the final hallway on the way to the classroom Kate is still sitting in. Instructor Sanchez stops at the corner and nods curtly to me, gesturing that I'm to continue alone. That's my cue. Scarlet gives my hand a squeeze before releasing it, and Justin grimaces at me.

Here we go.

I walk down the hallway alone in silence. I notice the alarm has stopped. *When did that happen?* I wonder vaguely.

Three doors to go.

My thoughts drift to the rest of my classmates and the students in the cafeteria. What are the headmasters telling them? What did Instructor Sanchez tell the headmasters exactly?

Two doors to go.

I wonder what movies are even playing that I could take Scarlet to for our first date. The civilized world outside of school seems so far away.

I'm outside the door.

I don't take a deep breath. I don't brace myself in any way. I just step into the doorway. Kate immediately comes into view. She's still sitting on that same desk where we observed her on the security footage.

"Kate?" I say cautiously, approaching her. "Kate, it's me, Ryan." I stop a few feet away from her.

She lifts her head as though she hadn't heard me approach. Her eyes are bloodshot and wet as though she's been crying. That's unexpected. I was prepared for the gloating, arrogant girl that Scarlet and Justin described from their interviews with her a few hours ago.

"Ryan," she says, and her voice cracks. "I thought they would send Scarlet."

"Yeah, me too, actually," I say. "But here I am."

She sniffs and wipes at her eyes with her palms. "You must be so mad at me," she says, and more tears fall gently down her cheeks.

"Kate, you've hurt a lot of people. Of course, people are upset. What did you expect?" I'm not sure if her tears are a ploy or not, to try to get me to feel for her, but white-hot anger bubbles inside me. She has no right to be crying over people being angry after what she has done. She has no right pretending to be a victim after all the stuff she's pulled.

"I know," Kate says, tears coming in earnest now. She makes no effort to wipe them anymore. "But you don't know the whole story."

"The whole story? Are you kidding me right now?" My voice is starting to rise, and I catch my temper and keep it in check. "You hit your best friend over the head with a pipe and gave her a concussion. Was she ever even your friend? You played Justin like a musical instrument and then tossed him aside when you were done with him. You led us on a wild goose chase through the sewers and into the desert. You killed someone!"

She flinches at the accusations I fling at her. Good. Let her feel a fraction of the pain that she's inflicted on innocent people for the past two—*or is it three?*—days.

"I didn't kill anyone," Kate whispers. "But you have to know the whole story. There's more to it than that."

"Somebody is dead," I hiss. "Who was that body in the sewers? Did you do that?"

"It's a townie," Kate says, her shoulders shaking with sobs. "I didn't know him. I don't know exactly who it is, but I didn't kill him. Please, Ryan, you have to hear me out. It's not what you think."

I inhale through my nose and out through my mouth as I consider the pathetic spectacle in front of me. How can she think that I will feel sorry for her after all she's done? How can she think that these tears will sway my opinion of her after she's bashed her roommate over the head and left her? After she cast Justin aside without a concern in the world? But do I think she killed someone? Do I believe she's telling the truth there?

I pause for a moment. Breaking up with someone is one thing. Knocking someone unconscious is one thing. But murder? That is a pretty big line to cross.

Kate looks up at me again, gasping between sobs. "What would my motive be for murder?" she says tearfully. "C'mon, you know it doesn't make any sense." She swallows thickly and glances around her. "I need your help. That's why I stayed. I'm—I'm in trouble."

I raise an eyebrow at her as questions whirl through my brain even more quickly now.

"What kind of trouble?" I ask warily.

"The headmasters, this whole school—it's not what you think it is."

What?

"It's part of a government organization," Kate goes on. "They recruit kids like us. Abandoned kids. Broken kids."

My mind drifts to my sister.

"They make it so that this school is all we have left in the world. So that this school is our everything. They brainwash us, Ryan. They manipulate us. They say we're going to stop crimes, that we're helping to preserve a functioning society. But the truth? The truth is that this school is the one that has messed up society in the first place! We don't fight criminals. We *are* the criminals."

Chapter Thirteen
THE ULTIMATE PRICE

SCARLET

C'mon, Ryan. What's taking him so long?

Instructor Sanchez and Justin had retreated into the classroom next to the one Ryan and Kate occupied. Justin is supposed to be ready to enter through the next window over if needed. I was left in the hallway alone.

I cannot take my eyes off the door as we wait for him to come out. My foot wriggles, aching to tap, and my mind buzzes with question after question. *Did it work? Is he okay? Is Kate okay?* My training pushes down the impulse to burst through the door myself, and I swallow and slowly exhale through my nose. *Be cool, Scarlet, be cool.* Ryan's got this. He has to. I refuse to think of the alternative.

I bite my lip and flex my fingers, ready to grab a weapon and go barging into that room the moment I even think I might hear Ryan's distress signal.

C'mon, c'mon. Why is it taking him this long? I blow another deliberate exhale out through my nose in an attempt to calm my thoughts and racing heart.

What a day. What a long, long few days. It's hard to imagine that only two days ago, I was just me, just Scarlet. Scarlet, who had a roommate named Kate and who was crushing on a cute guy named Ryan and annoyed by this dude named Justin. Now, Kate is my enemy, Justin is my brother (supposedly), and Ryan is my maybe-boyfriend. How the past couple of nights have changed my relationship with everyone is crazy. Things will never be the same. And we still have to apprehend Kate—I stare harder at the door Ryan went through—but I have a sense of finality, that this is it. That we are nearing the end of this particular chapter that has been filled with so many twists and turns.

I cannot help but wonder what will happen next. Right now, it's all so hard to process. So much has happened, so much had been simmering below the surface and building up to this moment. The Captures student in me was suspicious, so suspicious that Kate was able to fly below the radar for so long. Everyone knows how intense the training and screening process is to get into this school, so how was Kate able to fly by? How did the teachers and the headmasters not have a clue? How was it that the body in the sewers was the first thing that opened their eyes to Kate?

I frown and lick my lips. Maybe the school was caught just as off-guard as I was.

But for some reason, I don't think so. This is *Captures* after all—the academy that trains the highly elite forces responsible for capturing and taking in criminals. How could they miss a criminal right under their noses?

The back of my neck prickles uncomfortably. Something isn't adding up. Where are the rest of the teachers besides Instructor Sanchez right now anyway? Presumably guarding the rest of the student body, which they evacuated for their "safety" . . . Is it strange they kept Ryan, Justin, and me involved? That they letting us stay as part of the mission? I mean, we are part of the Final Four.

I rub my temples. This is too much for my concussed brain to think about right now. Adrenaline pumps through my body, making my legs and arms tingle. I am ready for action. So ready.

There's movement at the door, and I tense, ready to draw my weapon and go in guns blazing if Ryan is in danger.

He slowly steps out of the room, Kate behind him with her hands up.

"It's me. Stand down," Ryan calls gently from the door. "It's me, Scarlet." He searches my face, and I relax my stance just a millimeter.

"You have her in custody?" I call to him.

Beside him, Kate rolls her eyes, her hands still in the air. "I'm right here, you know," she snips at me. I'm both irritated and a little impressed by her bold sarcasm when she is clearly the low woman on the totem pole at the moment.

"Scarlet," Ryan says, his eyes still locked on mine. Shouldn't he be paying more attention to Kate at the moment? "Scarlet, we have to talk."

I stare blankly at him for a second. "Ryan," I say slowly, "I don't think now is a good time for that. But, believe me, I do want to talk. I think we need to take care of her first." I jerk my head toward Kate, who rolls her eyes again.

"No, we need to talk now," Ryan insists.

What's going on? What does he want to talk about? I assume our relationship status? That's the only thing that's changed between us in the last few hours. But now? Here?

I gaze at Ryan, searching his expression for a clue. His face is open, his eyes earnest. He doesn't appear to be under duress. Kate still has her hands in the air, so it doesn't seem like she has a weapon at his back. Has Kate tricked him somehow? Only one way to find out.

"Okaaay," I slowly agree. "Okay, let's talk. I'm reaching for my radio now." I move my hand toward the walkie-talkie clipped to my belt.

"No!" Ryan shouts then remembers himself. "I mean, no, I—we—need to talk first. Can you just hold off on calling the others right now? It's better if it's just you."

My frown deepens. "You know that's against protocol. You know that's not how we do things at Captures."

"Screw Captures!" Kate erupts suddenly. "Scarlet, just

forget about Captures for one freaking moment." She shakes her head and waves her hands in the air. "Look, I am completely unarmed, and I have no intent to harm you. Just hear us out for a second, and then you can call for your precious backup if you want. Come on. Please?"

Wait, did she just say, "hear *us* out?" Is Ryan working with her now? Thoughts zoom quickly in my head, one after the other, swirling together into an incoherent mass. I have way too many questions and way too few answers.

"Please, Scarlet," Ryan says. "Just give us a minute."

"Okay," I say. "Okay, you have one minute."

Ryan looks meaningfully at me and steps back inside the classroom. Kate follows him, throwing a nasty look over her shoulder at me.

I hope I'm not making a big mistake. I sigh deeply and follow them inside. If things turn sour, I can quickly give my distress signal and Instructor Sanchez and Justin would come to provide backup. But right now, I need answers.

"What's going on?" I ask. "Ryan, are you okay? Did she do something to you? Why are you acting this way?"

"Again, right here," Kate snipes.

"Look, Scarlet, we don't have a lot of time," Ryan says quickly. "Captures isn't what it seems. It isn't what you think it is."

"Did she hit you in the head or something, Ryan?" I quickly scan it for any wounds. Something must have messed up his brain.

"Scarlet, just stop. Put aside your hate and anger for me and just freaking listen," Kate says. Her cheeks are pink and her eyes are dark. "Captures isn't a crime-fighting school. We don't fight criminals. We are the criminals."

I look from Ryan to Scarlet. This has to be a joke. A really bad joke.

"Captures is part of a government organization," Kate continues before I can open my mouth to say anything. "They recruit kids like us, kids that show potential, and train us to take down their enemies to keep themselves powerful. Those plots and missions we go on during training? Those bad guys we take down? They're just people, Scarlet. They are just people who are trying to do good and protect their community. It's we who are the bad guys. Us. We are the bad guys, Scarlet."

Kate's voice rings loudly in my ears, and it's all I can hear. *We are the bad guys.* My vision swims, and I take a sudden seat on top of a desk. This can't be true. This can't be real. It has to be some lie of Kate's.

But deep down, I know there has to be a kernel of truth. Because something had struck me as just a little off too. I felt it. I felt the uneasiness. *But that's just the nature of Captures, right?*

"Scarlet," Ryan says, putting his face in front of mine, placing his hands on my cheeks. "Scarlet, are you with me? Are you following?"

I blink at him a few times and his face comes into focus. I swallow, hard. "Okay," I whisper. "Okay, keep talking."

The feeling of Ryan's warm hands on my face grounds me, keeps me from slipping into shock from this revelation, a revelation that I had already begun feeling, intuitively knowing deep in my bones.

"Captures is connected to the government. The government runs this place," Ryan repeats as if hearing it again will help it sink in. "And the headmasters are their puppets, spies that keep this place running and report our every move to the higherups. Didn't you ever think it strange that we have multiple headmasters? They're all spies. Every one of them. They need to divide up the duties of running the school and gathering intel for the government."

I open and close my mouth several times before I can manage words. "Why though? What's the point?"

Ryan and Kate glance at each other. "It's all about power," Ryan answers softly. "It's all about power for them. They pay for this school, for all this school's resources, with taxes the townies pay. The taxes are high. I mean, look at this place. Look at all the technology we have here, just at the school. How expensive it is! How did you think it was paid for?"

I don't answer because I'm ashamed to admit I hadn't ever given it a thought. Perhaps I noticed when I first arrived at Captures, coming from nothing, coming from the streets. But it just became part of my life, a fact about a place that eventually felt to me like home.

"Scarlet, the people we capture are dissenters. People who speak out against the harsh taxes, who speak out against the power that the government has. Those are our targets," Ryan continues. "Think about it. The constant surveillance. The guns. All the weapons. The government—and Captures—is spying on its own people to stay one step ahead of the game."

What game? I wonder. What is the game?

"They use us to do their dirty work," Kate finally chimes in, "so they don't have to get blood on their hands and can appear blameless and innocent. They put the blood on our hands instead."

Ryan takes a deep breath and closes his eyes. "Scarlet, you have to believe her. It sounds so crazy, but it makes sense. My sister . . ." Ryan swallows back his emotions. "They took my sister."

Kate puts her hand on Ryan's back, and I'm taken aback by the show of compassion. Her face is all twisted, looking like she's close to tears herself.

"My sister," Ryan chokes out. "My sister was a dissenter. She loved our community. She spoke out against the government, and they took her."

Kate bows her head and continues making slow circles on Ryan's back.

"How do you know?" I ask.

Ryan took a deep breath. "It was my aunt that turned her in. My aunt was working for the government, and she turned in her own niece. Her own family, Scarlet!" Ryan's voice breaks and tears leak out of his eyes.

Unbelievable.

"Are you—are you sure?" I stammer, though I don't doubt that Ryan's grief is real.

It's Kate who answers my question, though. "We're telling the truth. I'm part of the dissenters, Scarlet. I was recruited before I came to this school. I was going to be a spy for them here at Captures. We knew about Ryan's aunt. She was high up in the government. When Ryan's sister went missing, we suspected that she had something to do with it. I was there when she died. We killed her."

Ryan's shoulders shake in silent sobs, a dam of emotion breaking that he doesn't bother to hold in any longer. How could he? So much pain is bursting forth from him. His breath comes in gasps and tears earnestly streak down his cheeks. Kate's protective arm pulls him closer to her, and I'm strangely grateful for the comfort that she provides to him, to the boy I might love. Kate looks at me and something strange, something dark, flashes behind her eyes. How long has she been a part of this? I wonder what she's been through, how much her past has had an impact on her, and what thoughts must be running through her head now. My heart suddenly swells in empathy for her. She's just a kid. Ryan's just a kid. We're all just kids.

And even though there's so much to unpack here, my heart says that Ryan is telling the truth. That his grief is earnest. That Kate's words are too.

But there's still the chance I'm just being stupid for believing them.

"And the dead body in the sewers?" I ask, turning to Kate. "How do you explain that?"

Kate spoke up. "It was a townie. I don't know who he was. You have to understand that I am not the one pulling the strings around here. Everything is so much bigger than him. So much bigger than us. It's even bigger than Captures. We're talking about the government here. What's one townie in the scope of all that?"

She was right, I suppose. But it did not escape me that Kate had not answered the question. Or the fact that my head still hurt where she had hit me. Were these the actions of the kind of deranged criminal I thought Kate was? Or maybe just the actions of a scared teenager? Was it shame that I detected in Kate's expression too? Did she regret everything that had happened between us?

"Look, Scarlet," Kate says, looking seriously at me. Her eyes are bloodshot, and her hair is frazzled. This feels like an authentic Kate, like the friend I once had. Not a veneer, not a snarky and sarcastic mask, but a truly emotional girl. "I didn't know whose side you were on. I didn't know if I could trust you. You're part of the Final Four and so into Captures's plots, so into Captures's mission. Hurting you is one of my biggest regrets. I wish so much that I hadn't done that. I wish so much that we were still friends. Our friendship was real. It was so real for me, Scarlet." She swallows thickly. "And it kills me to know that you might not ever believe me. Just know that, even if you don't believe me, even if you don't want to be my friend, I get it. But I will never forget about you Scarlet. You weren't just my roommate; you were my best friend, and I will always treasure our time together." Her last few words come out in an impassioned rush. She practically gulps in air as they finish tumbling from her mouth, as though she hadn't dared to take even a single breath while speaking.

The lingering doubts I have about Kate vanish. I must make a choice, and I choose to trust her and Ryan. If this whole thing is really bigger than our school, bigger than her and me, then they are going to need as many friends and allies as they can get. It will take time to rebuild full trust between Kate and me, I decide. After all, my head still hurts quite a lot right now. But Kate has talent, and life is better with her on my side. Even if we aren't best friends or as tight as we used to be, maybe we can at least give being non-enemies a shot.

"I forgive you, Kate," I say quietly. "You have work to do. I can't trust you a hundred percent yet, but I'm willing to try. I'm willing to put the past behind us and try."

Kate responds with a watery laugh and jumps toward me, wrapping me in a hug. "Thank you," she says into my ear. "Scarlet, you have no idea how much this means to me. Thank you so much.

I look at Ryan over Kate's shoulder, and he smiles at me and nods. And I know I'm doing the right thing.

Kate releases me and looks between Ryan and me. "Are you ready?" she asks us.

I nod seriously. "Let's take down some bad guys."

—⟨⟩—

I radio Justin first.

"Scarlet! What the heck is going on? What's taking so long? Why did you go in the classroom too? Is Ryan okay? Is Kate okay?"

"Justin," I said calmly. "Chill, bro. Chill. I'm fine. Ryan is fine. But there's some stuff we have to tell you." I lower my voice to say this next part. "Are you alone?"

Justin doesn't answer for a minute, and I imagine he's trying to work out the puzzle of my question. "I mean, Instructor Sanchez is here," he says in a low voice.

"Just step outside in the hall for a minute. She can't overhear what we're about to tell you."

—⟨⟩—

Justin takes the news surprisingly well, or so it seems. He doesn't ask too many questions, but maybe he understands that now is not the time. There will be time to ask questions later, but now is the time for action. Because right now, we need to get Kate out of this school and back to the dissenters. Justin walks back inside the classroom where Instructor Sanchez waits.

"So everyone is clear on the plan?" Ryan asks nervously.

"Yes," I answer, surprisingly patient. I can't blame him for his nerves. We're about to play spy in an elite academy that specifically trains its students to sus out spies. I'm nervous too. My heart beats a steady *thump, thump, thump* in my chest, and I bite my lip.

It's game time.

I glance at my watch. It's 7:05 a.m. What happens next is a blur.

The three of us exit the classroom, and I pick up my radio once more, this time to contact Instructor Sanchez.

"Are you ready?" she asks immediately. "Do you have her in custody?"

"Yes," I say. "We have her. We're on our way back now."

For this to be convincing, we each must act our part. Kate is in handcuffs, and Ryan walks behind her, aggressively pushing her forward. I take the lead, walking us back to Instructor Sanchez and Justin. Kate keeps her head down. I'm sure the feeling of the cold steel around her wrists isn't a comfortable one, but she's got no choice now. Her fate is entirely in our hands.

When we arrive at the room where Instructor Sanchez and Justin are waiting, they meet us at the door.

Instructor Sanchez appraises us for a moment. How can she be a criminal? How can she be complicit in this school's corrupt activities? I swallow.

"Good," she says shortly. "You did it. Well done, the two of you."

"Thank you, Instructor Sanchez," I remember to say. "Permission to take the suspect into the holding cells?"

"Granted," Instructor Sanchez says.

I swallow again and paste a bland expression on my face. I can't look too happy about this. I'm merely doing my duty, after all.

We turn to leave, but before I can exhale a sigh of relief, Instructor Sanchez calls me back. "Scarlet, one moment."

Ryan and I exchange a look.

"Close the door, please," Instructor Sanchez says mildly.

"I—um," I stammer. Wordlessly, Instructor Sanchez closes the door herself, and the last thing I see is Ryan's panicked expression.

Please, I pray, *please, just stick to the plan.*

"Is something the matter, Instructor Sanchez?" I ask nervously. Is she on to us? She never uses my first name.

"Have a seat," she says, gesturing to an office chair behind me. She sits down herself, and wordlessly, I sink into a chair.

Am I about to be interrogated?

"I want to see how you are doing, Scarlet," Instructor Sanchez says, her eyes level with mine. "I know this can't be easy for you. Your roommate and former friend is suspected of committing some very serious crimes."

My eyes widen in surprise. I'm not quite sure where this is going, but I'll follow Instructor Sanchez's lead. How deep into this is she?

"Yes," I say slowly. "Yes, it's been tough."

Instructor Sanchez nods. "I bet. Having someone close to you betray your trust, committing such horrible atrocities right under our noses. Scarlet, the school administration has been keeping an eye on Kate for some time now. We suspected something like this might happen. We just didn't expect it to happen so soon." She looks down, and for a moment, she looks genuinely regretful. "We should have removed you from the situation sooner, Scarlet. And for that, we are sorry. You never should have gotten tangled up in this."

My mouth works in confusion. What is she saying? How much do they know?

"I . . . thank you. Hindsight is twenty-twenty," I say weakly.

Instructor Sanchez stares intently at me, putting one hand on each of my chair's armrests. "If there's anything, anything at all that we can do to make it up to you, to show just how sorry we are . . ." She lets her offer hang in the air.

Ah, it's starting to click into place now. Guilt. They feel guilty that I got hurt. That they knew Kate was up to something but didn't act quickly enough. And now they must be afraid that one of their star students, one of their Final Four, is going to have hard feelings about it. How could I use this to my advantage?

"Well," I say, "there is one thing."

Ten minutes later, I'm walking to the garage with keys to one of the SUVs in my hand.

"Scarlet," Justin hisses on the radio. "Scarlet, where the heck are you?"

I smile. "Meet me in the garage. The plan is still a go."

Five minutes after that, Justin, Ryan, and a still-handcuffed Kate are in the garage with me. They look from me to the running SUV in confusion.

"I don't understand," Ryan says slowly.

I grin broadly at him. "The perks of being roommates with someone the school thinks is a homicidal maniac. This is their hush payment to me to keep quiet about everything. They gave me access to vehicles and permission to leave campus."

"Well, I guess this is much easier than stealing a vehicle," Justin says, shrugging. "Let's go."

"Wait a minute," Kate says. "Aren't you forgetting something?" She jangles her handcuffs behind her.

"Right, it's time." Ryan takes the key to the handcuffs out of his pocket and uncuffs her. She gingerly rubs her wrists, and I feel a slight pang of guilt at the sight of the red welts encircling them. No time for that now, though.

We pile into the vehicle and set off toward one of the dissenter hideouts. Everything is going to plan.

The moment we arrive in the city, our plan falls apart.

Our SUV passes a checkpoint, and sirens start blaring. What the heck is this?

"New security measures!" Kate yells from the back seat. "We're breaking city curfew!"

The loud siren is accompanied by a flashing light and a mechanical voice shouting, "Exit your vehicle now! We are armed! Exit your vehicle now! We are armed!"

I swear loudly as professional capturers start appearing from the darkness around our SUV.

There is a loud knock on my window, and I look into the barrel of a gun. "Open up," the armed capturer says. "No one has to get hurt. Come out with your hands up."

"How much farther to the hideout, Kate?" Ryan asks frantically. "Can you make a break for it?"

"It's on the other side of the city," Kate wails. "This checkpoint isn't supposed to be here!"

"Look, we don't have a choice," Justin yells over the sirens. "You're gonna have to run for it."

"Open up, or I will break in this window," the capturer says again, tapping the butt of his gun against it to make sure I get the point.

"Okay," Kate says in a small voice. "Okay."

"I'm coming out," I say and lift my hands to show that I'm unarmed. He doesn't have to know about the knives under my shirt and strapped around my calves.

I slowly open the door, and the man outside my window takes a step back. Ryan, Justin, and Kate follow suit, and I hear their doors swing shut.

"What is the meaning of this? This is a Captures-issued vehicle, but we have no word that any vehicles have clearance or that Captures has a mission going," the guard says, glancing at the three of us. Wait, the three of us? I try to count from my periphery. Yes! It's just Justin and Ryan. Where is Kate?

"I can explain," I say without thinking. But then I realize that I have nothing to say. No excuses prepared. Stealing the vehicle and talking Instructor Sanchez into letting us bring Kate to her holding cell was supposed to be the hard part of the plan. This part was supposed to just be us riding off into the sunset, into freedom.

Suddenly, there is a loud gunshot, and the guard falls down. I drop to the ground and cover my head out of instinct. I've heard gunfire before, but this is so loud, so close, and so *real*.

More shots fire, and I frantically crawl back toward our vehicle. All I have are my knives, and everyone knows not to bring a knife to a gunfight. Have the dissenters come for us? Have they come for Kate, for one of their own?

I scramble under the car as chaos erupts. More gunfire, smoke bombs, boots running, and people falling down injured or worse. Blood coats the streets. It's an all-out assault. How did we walk right into this?

And then it dawns on me.

We walked right into this.

It was a trap. *A setup.*

Another capturer goes down, and I cover my mouth with my hand to stop from screaming as his blank eyes stare at me, unblinking, and life gushes from his nose and mouth as red streams of liquid.

The capturers are going down. Hard.

I hear a voice call out among the screaming, the cries of pain, and the unimaginably loud gunfire.

"Kate!"

I lift my head and peer through the smoke, zeroing in on a masked figure between two buildings, pointing at the SUV above me, and gesturing frantically toward the alley.

The door above me opens, and a pair of teenaged-girl-sized feet jump out. Without thinking, I reach out and grab Kate's ankles. She's not expecting me to be hiding under the vehicle, and she goes down.

Before she can start kicking, I scramble out from under the SUV.

"You traitor!" I scream at her, straddling her to hold her down. "How could you!" White-hot anger licks at my insides and spots form in my vision.

"I didn't have anything to do with this," Kate cries, thrashing. "Let me go. I have to go. You can still get away. The capturers don't know you're with me. The dissenters are here to rescue *me*. Grab the others and get away while you can!"

"You've told so many lies that I'm never going to believe a word that comes out of your mouth!" I yell.

"You don't have to believe me," Kate says, still thrashing. "You just need to let me . . . go!" And with that, she gives a great shove. Her push moves me off balance, and I go flying off of her. Like lightning, Kate is up and running toward an alley.

I let out an incoherent shout of rage and frustration and take off after her. I don't see any sign of Justin or Ryan, and I hope they are okay. They're Final Four too, and I pray their training has taken over and they are able to get away safely. I press my lips together. *Please, please let them not get caught in the crossfire.* Our training has prepared us for fighting dissenters, but nothing could have prepared me for the all-out battle unfolding around me.

Gunfire fills my ears. Smoke obscures my vision. Adrenaline fills my veins. The most jarring thing of all is the bodies. Fighting bodies. Injured bodies. Dead bodies. I'm not even sure who are the good guys and who are the bad guys anymore. *I'm not even sure what good and bad mean.*

"Kate, stop!" I yell, sprinting after her. To my surprise, Kate glances back at me and slows down once she reaches the alley.

The alley is deserted. The sounds of the raging battle just outside its boundaries are strangely muted.

I spot Ryan, lying alongside a dumpster, panting heavily, a great gash dripping blood down his forehead. Justin is kneeling next to him, gently blotting the injury to stop the bleeding. They look how I feel. Both are breathing heavily, white as ghosts. How could our plan have gone *this* wrong? How could we have walked right into this? We are trained to take down criminals—dissenters, I remind myself—but for all-out war? I'm not sure that any amount of training would have readied us for this.

"Kate is a traitor. She set this up," I yell to them.

"You don't know what you're talking about, Scarlet," Kate says in a low voice, a dangerous voice.

"How did they know then, Kate? How did your group of dissenters know that we would be here? That these capturers would all come out of their bases to investigate a 'stolen' Captures vehicle? You set it up. You set it all up; just admit it. You've been the master manipulator this whole time, and we're just your puppets!" Blood pounds in my ears.

Ryan and Justin are silent, and Kate assesses me with cold eyes. Why won't she admit it? Why keep up this stupid charade?

"Kate," Ryan says quietly from the ground. "Is it true?"

For a moment, the expression on Kate's face slips, and she looks like a scared little girl. Then the mask is back up.

"Yes," she says softly. "It's true. I set this up. But I didn't mean for you to get caught in the crossfire. I meant what I said back there in the classroom, Scarlet. I meant it. We didn't know about the new checkpoint. We were meant to get outside the city, for the capturers to tail us and for us to ambush them there."

"Then why are all the dissenters here?" I hiss.

"They were tailing us. There were following us to protect us," Kate says, looking down.

I know it's stupid. I know it goes against all my training, but I want so badly to believe her. Maybe she really is just a small part, a young girl who just got caught up in something so much bigger than herself.

Behind Kate, on the other side of the alley, movement catches my eye. My fingers tense, ready to grab my knives. Kate hasn't noticed. She's looking between me and Ryan and Justin, still kneeling on the ground.

"It wasn't supposed to be like this," she says sadly.

There are two figures behind Kate now, about thirty feet back. I squint through the smoke, trying to make out which side they are on. Are they dissenters? Capturers?

Suddenly, there is movement behind me, and I flinch. I whirl around, grabbing a knife from my belt.

Instructor Sanchez.

I nearly drop my knife in surprise. "Instructor Sanchez? What are you doing here?" I gasp.

"Put the knife down, Scarlet," she says evenly, her eyes fixed on Kate standing behind me. "We're not here for you. And here." She tosses a roll of bandages over to Ryan and Justin, and Justin immediately starts wrapping it around Ryan's wound to staunch the bleeding.

"How did you find us?" I ask stupidly.

"Capture's's vehicles all have tracking in them. I thought your request for a car was suspicious, and I was right. Kate,

I don't know how you keep escaping, but it's over. It's all over now."

I'm so busy gaping at Instructor Sanchez that I nearly forget about the approaching figures behind Kate.

"You're surrounded. You're done," Instructor Sanchez says with finality. Kate spins around, and the figures behind her, capturers, come into clear view, their guns leveled at her. "Nobody else has to get hurt on your account. Come on."

Kate hesitates, and I can practically see the cogs in her mind turning, desperate to put together a plan.

"If I come quietly, will I be safe?" Kate asks.

"Yes," Instructor Sanchez says without hesitation. "You will not be harmed. Come, Kate. No one has to get hurt," she repeats.

Kate lowers her head, and she looks like a girl defeated. It's really over for her now. I wonder what kind of desperate plan she's formulating in her head. And I wonder how Instructor Sanchez, how the capturers, can actually be the criminals Kate claims them to be.

She walks slowly over to us, to me and Instructor Sanchez, with her hands hanging loosely at her sides. The two capturers behind her keep their weapons trained on her as if they expect her to make a move.

Kate is three steps away from me when a loud gunshot rings through the alleyway. Kate reaches out and grabs me, spinning me in front of her.

What the heck?

The gunshot still ringing in my ears, I feel a warm wetness in my stomach, and I glance down. A bright red patch blossoms on my shirt, growing larger and larger, and then the pain hits me.

I've been shot.

I touch the blood gushing out of me experimentally, as though I'm not sure what blood is like. It's hot and wet and sticky and *mine*. There's so much of it.

I gasp and slide down to the dirty ground of the alley. My vision starts to go dark, and I feel lightheaded. People around me are shouting, I think, but I don't really hear them. I don't hear anything.

With fading eyes, I look up at the dark night sky, which begins to blur. My lungs start to give out, and my heart steadily quiets its pace. A single tear rolls down the side of my cheek as I struggle for a breath.

The last thing I see is a shadowy figure walking out of the dark alley.

EPILOGUE

SCARLET
Murderer by night, friend by day.

Deep in the sewer, your life in disarray.

I open my eyes. Endless commotion plagues my mind in a way I have never experienced before. My thoughts are like bullets, flying by me for split seconds, only to be forgotten again, shaking me to my core, relentlessly pounding my whole body until my lungs give out. Suddenly, memories overwhelm my battered brain, and an avalanche of emotions sweeps over me.

Nothing is real. Nothing is what it appears to be, I frantically think to myself. And for the first time, I begin to question who I truly am. That's the one secret I'm not sure I'll ever figure out.

But one thing I know for certain.

I will seek revenge.

ABOUT THE AUTHOR

Allison Moores lives in sunny California. *Murderer's Blade* is her debut novel. When not writing, Allison enjoys traveling, reading, and hanging out with her three standard poodles and a tiny Yorkie named Mango.

A free ebook edition is available with the purchase of this book.

To claim your free ebook edition:

1. Visit MorganJamesBOGO.com
2. Sign your name CLEARLY in the space
3. Complete the form and submit a photo of the entire copyright page
4. You or your friend can download the ebook to your preferred device

Morgan James BOGO™

A **FREE** ebook edition is available for you or a friend with the purchase of this print book.

CLEARLY SIGN YOUR NAME ABOVE

Instructions to claim your free ebook edition:
1. Visit MorganJamesBOGO.com
2. Sign your name CLEARLY in the space above
3. Complete the form and submit a photo of this entire page
4. You or your friend can download the ebook to your preferred device

Print & Digital Together Forever.

Snap a photo   Free ebook   Read anywhere